# Noelle's
# Christmas
# Wedding

The Candy Cane Girls, book 1

## Bonnie Engstrom

Dear Reader ~

I hope you will enjoy this series that tells the stories of women who are what I call super friends ~ friends who committed as teenagers to prayer and loyalty bound by a moniker. The Candy Cane Girls are a unique group of sister friends. I hope their stories will inspire other young women.

In fact I am hoping to start an inspiration, a situation or a way to encourage young women, especially teen girls, to write their own stories. I have three teenage granddaughters who are bright and talented but as far as I know do not record their thoughts and experiences. I also pray for other teen girls of friends. Still it troubles me they are not writing about their lives and experiences. Please join me in praying for an upcoming of young women writers.

As you read through this series, and I hope you will, please note how each book tells a story about individual women, how each struggle with a personal situation and overcomes it. Some of the circumstances each encounter are destined by faith and fate; but all require belief and commitment to each other and to the faith of each. I hope you will read every story to see how Cindy deals with her new love's health issues, and Candy takes her fears into action, and Connie . . . well she has a problem that she overcomes with the help of sweet Jake, her 'problems solving' dog. Jake will appear in many following books. He was my running companion for many years – the dearest dog. But Lola and Happy Arthur are shining woofers in their own stories.

But wait until you get to Natalie and Melanie! They hold the keys to lasting friendship. Their stories are almost legendary.

All stories in the series can be read individually, but you will enjoy them more and understand them more if you read them in order.

Noelle, Cindy, Connie, Candy, Natalie, Doreen and especially Melanie will steal your heart.

You will have fun with the different wedding venues. How many weddings have you attended in an historical place, or in a hospital lobby or a gym? Maybe these will be your first and most memorable.

You will do me a great favor if you enjoyed this series and write a quick, honest review on Amazon or Goodreads. Just a few words mean a lot and encourage others to read it.

Thank you. If you would like to be connected to me for comments and conversation please sign up for my newsletter at www.bonnieengstrom.com and learn about my writing history. You can email me at bengstrom@hotmail.com. Please put SERIES <in caps) in the subject line. I would love to chat with you.

By the way, the Candy Cane Series is ideal for group discussion, especially for book clubs. I have a special offer for book clubs for all of my books. If you are interested please email me at bengstrom@hotmail.com with CLUB <all caps) in the subject line.

Blessings,

Bonnie

# *Chapter One*

Newport Beach, California

Noelle pumped on the brakes and surveyed the string of cars through the fog on her windshield. The sea mist was especially heavy this afternoon. She slammed her palm against the leather-covered steering wheel and gnawed on her lip. Why had she taken MacArthur Boulevard to the Coast Highway today? Is this the first day of the Christmas Boat Parade weekend? No, that's not until December. This is only the Friday before Thanksgiving – not yet holiday season.

Yet, it was in full swing. Must be stuff like the fifteen decorated Christmas trees for charity at the Fairmont Hotel and the special Thanksgiving event of the film festival. So much was always happening in this tourist town. Even Rogers Gardens had started its opulent annual boutique that attracted so many out of towners.

She had read about all the events in the Daily Navigator, but in her stressful frame of mind she'd forgotten. *I could have avoided Corona del Mar completely by taking surface streets and Newport Coast Drive. Still, I would have passed Rogers Gardens on San Joaquin Hills Road and had to deal with the tourist buses.* She gripped the steering wheel with damp hands. *Either way, I will be late for my appointment with the florist. I hate that.*

Jill, her now former wedding coordinator, said the florist was forgiving, but Noelle lived for punctuality. Her mother said she was a bit obsessive about it, but she didn't care. Being on time was a matter of courtesy. If only the faculty meeting hadn't lasted so long. Then the principal followed her to her car chatting and constantly touching her arm. Maybe she should have left early. But, as the new teacher that would have made her look bad. Canceling her wedding just a month before the planned date made her look bad enough.

The cars inched forward along Pacific Coast Highway, truly inched, giving Noelle no way to change lanes or get out of the mess. She would be at least twenty minutes late. Maybe thirty.

Finally! The Persian rug store and a few niche restaurants came into view, including Rothchild's. At last she was turning south. She passed the Starbucks at the corner of Marguarite Avenue where three tiny tables were crowded with bundled-up patrons each holding a dog leash, and amazingly, sleeping dogs. What gives with that? *Guess those people aren't going to any tourist events. Smart move.*

The light finally turned green and Noelle's little car crept past the Five Crowns Restaurant and through the last clogged intersection of Corona del Mar. Breathing a sigh of relief, she gunned the gas and sped past the open spaces. The endless Pacific Ocean on her right spouted huge waves that rolled in to spit up on the sand below the bluffs. It was a beautiful sight she never tired of, although she seldom saw it anymore. She passed the Sugar Shake Shack and memories flooded her brain. The girls from her swim team had pulled into the sand lot in front of it. They were tired and smelled of chlorine from the high school pool, but they'd won. Their relay team, dubbed the Candy Canes because of their red and white striped swimsuits, was responsible for Vista del Mar High School taking the All-state title. She'd thought Coach Douglas might have a heart attack, he was so excited. He'd hugged each of them, all the team members, not just the relay team, then slipped a twenty into each of the Candy Canes' hands.

"Celebrate, girls! Have fun – just be sure it's loaded with sugar, not alcohol."

Noelle had ordered a double-malt chocolate chip shake with triple whipped cream. It was a special day, a day of celebration and bonding. A day to remember.

Noelle finally pulled into the parking lot of the opulent hotel resort. She refused to have a valet park her shining red baby. Instead, she found a self-parking slot. The trek to the resort in the expansive lot seemed like miles in her spike-heeled shoes. *Another dumb thing. Should've switched to tennies since I'm not here to impress anyone.* Jill was meeting her there with some guy named Braydon, the florist contracted to provide the flowers for her now defunct wedding. *Does he know why we're meeting – to cancel the wedding contract? I hope Jill gave him a head's up. This is so embarrassing.*

Jill said he was the only florist in Southern California who could produce baby Calla Lilies in December – a desire of her now former mother-in-law-to-be, Gladys, who had carried them in her own wedding. Noelle felt a combination of relief and guilt for no longer being under the woman's persuasive thumb. She really hadn't cared what flowers she might have carried. She rubbed her arm hoping to diffuse the bruises. She'd read somewhere that would make them hurt less.

An attendant opened a huge glass door for her. She felt a bit dizzy. Maybe lunch would have been a good idea. Glancing about the enormous lobby she spotted Jill. Sweet Jill, not officious, not too glamorous, just right in her black slacks and starched white blouse. Jill held out her arms to hug Noelle, but as Noelle spread her own arms, she felt woozy and tripped, then landed in muscular ones. Just before she passed out she smelled the heady scent of roses.

~

Braydon Lovejoy had been rocking back and forth between his feet and silently praying. Trying

7

hard to be a patient man, he'd been praying extra hard lately for that quality as he waited to meet his client. Jill, the wedding coordinator, had gotten him very excited last month about this bride-to-be. The contract would mean a huge boost to his business, especially when the society section of the Daily Navigator newspaper featured the wedding – with his floral displays. Maybe he'd even be featured in the business section of Orange County NOW. He'd planned to tell the bride-to-be about his ideas for the attendants' bouquets. Brilliant red and pure white roses with petal edges dipped in sparkling silver glitter would make a stunning statement for a December wedding. Jill had told him the bridesmaids would wear red taffeta gowns with white sashes. Perfect! He visualized young women clutching the heart-shaped nosegays he'd designed. But, the pièce de résistance would be carried by the bride. He couldn't wait to see her face light up when he described it to her.

Jill arrived for their meeting as he'd finished wrapping a bouquet of Double Delights, his finest roses, in Cellophane. Grinning widely, he planned to present the woman he'd privately dubbed "Diva Day" with the expensive, intensely-perfumed blooms. He strode from his hotel satellite shop into the lobby with Jill trailing behind him sniffing audibly at the scent of the flowers. That Jill was such a card.

The strange expression on Jill's face had given him pause. She'd just started to whisper something about a surprise when a beautiful woman toppled into his arms.

He'd tried to toss the bouquet off to the side, but there was no time. The Double Delight roses crushed against his forearm sandwiched between his Alpaca sweater and a mane of chestnut hair. His first reaction was to wrap his arms firmly around the limp woman.

The roses finally slipped to the floor with a rustling of Cellophane wrap as he lifted the woman's prone form, not too gracefully, under her shoulders and dragged her onto one of the lobby's overstuffed sofas. Long, thick hair cascaded across her face like a shawl of sepia threads. He heard Jill murmuring behind him and turned to her for advice.

She raised her eyebrows and shrugged. Lacking any guidance he grabbed the recumbent woman's slim ankles and shifted them onto the sofa. Although he felt uncomfortable doing it, he fingered the strands of hair from her face, especially those caught in her open mouth. Reddish-brown eyes that matched the color of her hair flicked open wide. Her beautiful face twisted in fear. At least that was Braydon's first thought.

"Who?" The single word gurgled in the woman's throat like a clogged sink drain. Braydon couldn't shake off the feeling she was alarmed, maybe even panicked.

"Braydon Lovejoy. Miss Day?" He hoped his smile was warm and that he really addressed Noelle Day. He'd realized he'd risen and stood jingling the coins in his pockets.

Jill hadn't said if the woman who'd collapsed in his arms was her client. Jill seemed to be in a bit of shock herself. He heard her mumbling, then realized she was talking on her cellphone, and, of all the crazy things, saw her marching around the lobby clasping the cast off bouquet and ignoring his plight. He pondered briefly about the other hotel patrons in the lobby disregarding the scene. No one stepped forward to offer assistance.

"Ye – yes. Noelle Day." The voice was tiny, almost childlike. Not the voice of the diva he'd expected. Color crept across the delicate cheekbones in a pale pink flush not unlike a Maidens Blush rose in full bloom. Gingerly he lifted an icy hand into his large warm one. She yanked it back immediately to clasp its mate. Fear again? Or, simple embarrassment? Braydon knelt beside the sofa to whisper, hoping to reassure Noelle and answer her unspoken question.

"Miss Day," he began tentatively. "You tripped on a rug. I caught you. End of story. Are you all right?"

Suddenly, the woman swung her legs over the sofa edge, sat up tall, pushed a sleeve up to check her watch and spoke in a clipped voice. "Sorry I'm late, and so sorry for the trouble. You've been very kind. Now, can we get on with our meeting?" She was all business and spoke as if the fainting incident had never happened.

The softness he'd seen in her eyes after she'd passed out was gone. He'd been shocked to hear her formally enunciated words. "This wedding is not going to work out, Mr. Lovejoy. My *former* (she'd emphasized the word) fiancé and I have parted company." Her eyes took on saucer appearance as they perused him from head to toe. When she looked into his face again, she said, "Do you understand? I'm terribly sorry for any inconvenience, and I have a check for you to cover the cost of your time and effort. Per the contract." She whipped a cream colored paper out of her purse.

He nodded mutely, his eyes rooted to her oval ones, brownish pools of pain and sorrow. What made him feel empathy for this lovely creature? Was he reading too much into the sudden change in her demeanor?

Braydon noticed the tiny hands now resting on her legs were tightly clasped, pasty white. She rose to get up from the sofa and teetered for a second. He offered a hand that was ignored. It took every ounce of restraint not to salute.

# *Chapter Two*

"Today was my dumb day, Misty. Messed up everything. Maybe I am a stupid klutz." Noelle thought about how Clay her former fiancé frequently chastised her for doing what he'd called "stupid mistakes." Like forgetting where she'd placed her keys, not picking up the phone before the answering machine kicked in, even bowing her head in a restaurant to silently give thanks for the meal before her. That, he'd said, was so embarrassing, so intimidating to those who didn't believe. That was when she'd started covering her arms in long sleeves.

Two doe-like eyes looked sadly at Noelle. Without warning a wet tongue delivered a sloppy kiss across her nose. Noelle clasped the tiny soft body closer, snuggling the furry face into her neck. The longhaired Chihuahua's tail, almost the length of its ten-inch body, flipped furiously tickling her arm. "You are my best friend – maybe my only one." Glancing at her calendar to see what the next few days held, she revised her thoughts.

She hadn't made many friends among the other teachers at school, but that was . . . whose fault was it? Ultimately, it came down to hers for letting a man dictate her social life. Maybe meeting with her old high school buddies for their annual pre-holiday lunch and pedicure would make her feel better.

It was almost six years since they'd graduated. Most had won numerous academic and athletic awards, but none of those held their hearts as much as the swim relays. Seldom seeing her old friends, except for the annual group pedicure followed by luncheon at The Cannery Restaurant, she was thankful for the continued friendships. They'd all had such lofty dreams. Coach Douglas had called them his Princess Team, his dream team, because they'd pulled off so many wins with a perfectly synchronized relay. But, the girls had another idea. They would stick together as friends for the long haul, not just swim meets. They promised, they would keep in touch forever. And, so far, after six years, they had.

Noelle grabbed the red marker she kept near her calendar and embellished the following Saturday with a heart and superimposed it with a crude candy cane. Mentally, she planned out her clothes for the occasion. She'd have to wear long sleeves to cover the yellowing bruises, so she chose a red and white striped jersey. Perfect. Her arms would look like candy canes.

Braydon pushed through the scraggly blonde tufts at his aching temples with his thumbs. He couldn't believe the biggest wedding contract he'd ever hoped to have had been cancelled. Poof! It could have been his finest moment as a floral designer, his entré to be listed by wedding coordinators and upscale wedding venues on their "preferred lists." His first reaction was unbelief, actually a non-reaction. When Noelle told him the wedding was off, he thought at first she meant the date was changed. But, the russet eyes bore into him and made it clear. "Off, cancelled, kaput," were the words she spoke. "Is that clear?" He stood like chiseled stone, a marble statue, unable to move. He'd accepted the generous check and tucked it in his pocket. Later, he ripped it up. He didn't know why – just that it was the right thing to do. Maybe because he saw something in Noelle, something deep that disturbed him, something not even she was aware of. Something vulnerable . . . and beautiful.

He sat on the edge of his bed to pray.

~

Noelle stretched to position the fragile angel on top of the tree. She'd had to unfold the plastic step stool to reach the treetop. She'd considered a tabletop tree for her little condo, but Christmas was her favorite time of year, and she wanted to go "whole hog," as her uncle Mart would say. So, even though it was the night before Thanksgiving, she dug out her parents' castoff tree from her garage, the one they'd bought twenty-five years ago on sale at The Antique Guild. It took her three hours to assemble, then another to put on the seven strings of lights. The angel had tiny lights imbedded in her tulle skirt, and when Noelle turned the switch, she "awed." *So beautiful. Thank you, Lord, for giving me this reminder of your grace and holiness and coming to earth as a baby to save us.*

She stirred the mini-marshmallows floating atop her hot chocolate and sighed. In four weeks it would have been "the day," her wedding day. Staring into the electric fireplace she realized she had no regrets. Still, it was sad things turned out the way they did. God had given her the strength to break off the engagement and to move on. Would she ever have the courage to love again? She was looking forward to meeting the Candy Canes for their annual get-together in three days. Laughter and sharing old memories would be a balm for her wounded spirit. She took a sip of the steaming chocolate and massaged the yellowish bruise on her wrist, one of the last evidences of her former love.

~

Noelle was stepping out of the shower when the phone rang. Wrapping a towel around her she shivered and stood still to listen. "Call from cellphone C, A," the tinny voice repeated several times. Although the little window on the phone displayed the number, it wasn't one she recognized. As she reached for the phone to take the call, it disconnected. Well, if it was important the caller could have left a message on the answering machine or could call again. If she had time later she'd call back the number.

Slipping on her sandals she smiled at the tiny candy cane painted on her big right toenail. The group pedicure had been a major giggle session. Even the nail girls had been filled with mirth laughing and chatting among themselves in their native Vietnamese tongue.

Out of habit, she tucked the silver cross around her neck under the long sleeved jersey. This afternoon she would meet the Candy Canes for coffee in Fashion Island. But first she needed to stop at the stationary store to cancel the wedding announcements.

~

Braydon paced. He'd been up since five, sleep having escaped him. A path had formed in his carpet. He stared into the bathroom mirror for perhaps the tenth time. But, every time he looked, he saw not his own blue eyes, but the murky chocolatey ones of the woman who'd fallen into his arms. He was so distraught he missed church today, during Advent and right before Christmas, his favorite time.

Jill, his beloved wedding coordinator contact, had given him the woman's phone number – actually on the original contract for her December wedding - the one that was supposed to take place in several weeks. He'd attempted to call her about an hour ago, but no answer. He'd never misused or abused something like that before, but his feelings were so overwhelming, he made an exception. Feeling foolish, he hadn't left a message. *Maybe I should have, so she wouldn't think it was some random call from a weirdo.*

The ancient grandfather clock downstairs in the entry chimed ten times giving Braydon a nudge. His main shop in Corona del Mar opened at eleven on Sunday, so he'd better hurry.

Traffic, as usual in Corona del Mar, this small satellite town of Newport Beach, was creeping. Finally, he was able to turn off a side street to park behind Lovejoy's - The Love in Bloom Florist – next to the fancy stationary store. He always got a kick out of the name that Mom had come up with. Parking the floral delivery van a bit crooked in the last vacant spot, he decided to situate it better. He backed up and heard a huge crunching sound. Oh, no! He jumped out of the van, remembering to put it in park, and raced to the source of the sound – a shiny red BMW roadster with a dented passenger door and crushed front fender.

A woman with long brown hair cascading over her steering wheel was slumped forward. When he pounded on her door she raised a tear-stained face. Chocolate eyes swimming in pools of tears looked accusingly at him. He took a step back realizing who it was. The girl from the other day, the one who'd collapsed in his arms but refused his help.

# *Chapter Three*

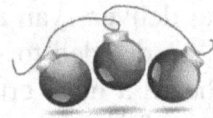

Noelle stumbled into her condo, kicked off her shoes and stripped off her clothes. What a horrible day; four days, no, four weeks actually. Four weeks ago telling Clay the wedding was off, and a few days ago telling the flower man that there will be no wedding, and today he backed his van into her precious car. On a Sunday! Maybe she was paying penance for not going to church this morning.

She dialed Cindy's number and cancelled the coffee date with the Candy Canes right now, after she got home from the accident fiasco. It was more than she could take, more than she wanted to explain. So embarrassing. Bad enough she had cancelled the wedding and they all still had bridesmaid dresses hanging in their closets. She would make it up to them, even if it took half a month's salary. Yet, she was blessed by their group love and understanding. She hadn't explained at the pedicure appointment yesterday exactly why the wedding was off. But, when Cindy grasped her arm in sympathy to show she cared, Noelle had winced. Cindy's eyebrows had raised in question, and her eyes held sympathy for her friend. Noelle had smiled feebly and shook her head slightly. Cindy squeezed her hand and nodded.

She raced upstairs attired only in her bra and panties. Half naked. Not like her at all. But, like a woman chased by demons.

Slipping on a long soft cotton shift and clutching her Bible to her chest, she felt much better. More centered. More human. She sat down on the side of her bed and curled her bare feet under her. Misty jumped up and licked her toes making her collapse in giggles.

"Silly girl. So funny." Noelle cuddled the little dog close to her chest. Her only true love who would never abandon her. "Thank you, sweet thing. I needed that."

Misty jumped down and settled in her fluffy dog bed. Noelle opened her Bible randomly and was surprised to be in John. She scanned through and a passage caught her eye. Maybe it was the word "truth."

But when he, the Spirit of truth, comes, he will guide you into all the truth. He will not speak on his own; he will speak only what he hears, and he will tell you what is yet to come. John 16:13

19

She clutched the pink Bible closer and sighed with such a loud whoosh of breath she alarmed Misty who raised her pointy little snout and woofed. She said, "It's okay, girl," but Noelle realized her voice was trembling.

She had finally accepted the truth about Clay. She remembered being so excited, actually overwhelmed, when he proposed that she'd dropped to her own knees to embrace him. His proposal had been so wonderfully traditional – down on one knee, a velvet box gleaming with a huge solitaire diamond that glittered wildly when he opened it. He slipped the gorgeous ring on her finger and kissed her hand. Her voice had trembled then, too. The whole scenario was everything she had dreamed since she had been thirteen. Now, at twenty-five, more mature, more worldly, more dependent on God instead of a man's fake fawning, she knew she had done the right thing breaking it off. If only she had gathered her courage months ago, instead of four weeks.

Her eyes focused on the last part of the scripture, "he will tell you what is yet to come."

"Really, God?" she whispered aloud startling Misty again. "That is almost like a prophecy. I'm sure I'm not prophetic; I don't believe prophesy is a gift You have given me. Teaching, maybe. I know that is one of Your gifts." She squeezed her eyes shut tight and envisioned rows of students in her class. How she loved them, and loved teaching. "Yes, teaching. Thank you.

"Now, Lord, please get me through this difficult period of my life. Give me the courage to move forward and to put behind all the ugliness. I know You have a hope and future for me, a good future, as Your Word says in Jerimiah 11. I know I'm not supposed to see it just now, but to trust." Shaking her head, she petitioned Him again. "Please, give me vision, and give me peace."

~

Noelle met with the insurance adjuster the next morning in front of her condo. Fortunately, she had been able to drive her little red car home. Still, it was very damaged. Thanks to Braydon the florist guy. It almost had to be towed here. Yet, as embarrassing as it was, it functioned. She thought about the tow truck guy laughing and showing her how to drive it. Short distances he said. Fortunately, she lived only a stone's throw from Vista del Mar High School where she taught English. But, she wasn't looking forward to all the comments and questions she would receive in the school parking lot.

# *Chapter Four*

"What the … happened, Noelle?" Bruce Walker, the principal, put his arm around her shoulder. She tried to shrug it off without being impolite, but his reaction to the damage on her little car was exactly what she expected, and dreaded. From other teachers, but not from him.

"Someone backed into me in a parking lot. Not a big deal, sort of a minor inconvenience."

"I hope you weren't hurt?" Bruce squeezed her shoulder more tightly than she would have liked. He had done that before after the faculty meeting, and even the day she was hired. She had tried to diffuse his actions then and hoped she'd succeeded. Obviously not.

"You look as lovely as always. Maybe a tad stressed." His grin crowded between his short gray beard and moustache. He squeezed her shoulder again and leaned closer to her, his coffee breath hanging next to her ear.

She pulled away. "Yes, thank you. Really, I am fine." She gave him a wobbly smile. "No big deal," she repeated. "But, thanks for asking." Noelle opened her trunk and lifted out her laptop case and the funny looking black patterned tote that held her class stuff – lesson plans, corrected papers, syllabus.

He wouldn't let it go. "Let me walk you in." He insisted, this time wrapping his arm around her waist. How could she refuse and offend the school principal?

She tried. "I'm really, really fine, Bruce. Thank you so much for caring." He didn't get the hint, no matter how strong her voice was, no matter how much she tried to pull away from him.

"NO! I want to escort you and be sure you feel safe."

She did not feel safe in his arms. He had tried many times to entice her to go out with him, until he learned she was engaged.

Gaining courage from her memory of Psalm 119 last night when she was sitting on her bedside with Misty, she pulled away. "Bruce," she said firmly, "I really appreciate your concern. But, I need to do this alone. Do you understand?"

Bruce pulled back. He appeared offended, but tried to hide it with another ear to ear smile showing gleaming teeth. (Probably implants, Noelle thought irreverently. Then giggled silently to herself. This man was such a phony.)

When another car pulled up, he finally released his hand from her waist. Noelle relaxed and audibly sighed, maybe too loud. Hoisting her laptop bag on her shoulder and grasping the tote bag, plus her over stuffed purse, she waved a thank you.

What? He was pursuing her?

"Noelle, wait. Please." The older man's voice had a leer in it. She stopped. After all, he is the principal of her school, her boss. She mustn't ignore his request.

*Please, God, may it be just to be sure I turn in my student evaluations. Not something personal.*

Bruce caught up with her. He was breathing hard. He grabbed her wrist and spun her around. "I am very worried about you, Noelle." His brow furrowed, and he looked directly into her eyes. "Let's talk this situation over dinner tonight. K?"

~

Noelle almost panicked. She wanted to get away from this persistent man. But, again she reminded herself that he is her boss. She forced a grin and said, "Sorry. Busy tonight, but thanks." But, what situation was he referring to? Her little accident?

She rushed ahead ignoring the heaviness of her laptop and tote and silly purse. Why did she keep so much in it? Waving to Carly Beasley the receptionist, she ran to her classroom and collapsed in her desk chair. Apparently, he wasn't close on her heels. Thank God he hadn't followed her. School district protocol implied, if not stated in a document, that principals should not enter a classroom without first announcing such to a teacher. It could set a teacher on edge and interrupt her lesson.

Her students filed in, took seats and looked at her funny. Was her makeup smeared? She knew her clothes were not tattered or in disarray. Finally, her boldest student, Josh, a nice kid, but one who had no problem speaking out, said, "You okay, Ms. Day?"

"Yes, Josh. Why do you ask?"

"Because your shoes are on the wrong feet and your watch is on the wrong hand. You are right-handed, aren't you?" Josh settled back in his chair with a grin. Mr. Confident. But, he was one of her best students, and she wasn't offended. She simply grinned back and giggled.

She switched her watch to her left hand and made a display of kicking off her shoes and transferring them to the other feet. It as a fun moment, and the class settled down, after a good laugh at her. And, she at herself. This, she reminded herself, was why she loved to teach, and how she teaches best. She felt a bond, an affinity with her students. Teaching them was so much fun, and she knew it was reciprocal.

~

Noelle parked the damaged BMW in an empty slot and traipsed into her condominium schlepping the tote and laptop, and also her heavy purse. Designer accoutrement or not, she had to get rid of it soon. Either empty it and dispose of stuff, or buy a new smaller one, one that couldn't possibly accommodate all her stuff – much of it unnecessary.

Her right shoulder was aching, had been for about a month. Purse? Possibly. Stress from the breakup. Probably. Maybe both.

But, it was the one Uncle Mart had bought for her on a whim at Bloomingdales. The one Clay, her former fiancé, wanted to buy for her, then criticized when Uncle Mart bought it for her.

She rubbed her left shoulder and upper arm. Why did they still hurt? It had almost been a month. When the Candy Canes learned about her 'situation,' as she called it, every girl praised her for having the courage to end the relationship. Although she finally had, the hurts were still there. In her heart and on her body.

She wandered into the kitchen for a soda and pushed the button blinking on her answering machine. Clay's surly voice penetrated the small room. "You can't do this, Babe. It's so embarrassing. Think about our parents, especially your mother." He was going for the jugular. Playing on sympathy for her mom. How phony! His voice driveled, almost like a panting dog salivating. "How will she ever hold her head up high again? How will you? Everyone will think you were unfaithful … because," he paused dramatically, "I will tell them that." He rambled on in a piercing voice. She pushed the delete message button on the machine and collapsed in a kitchen chair. A threat. How horrible was this man? This man she had claimed to love, almost for a lifetime. Her mind spun.

Why can't he leave me alone? I am no longer his. I made that very clear. The wedding was canceled. So were all the special things. The cake, the caterer, the venue, the program, even the flowers.

The flowers. Braydon. The man who ran into my car. The kind man who rescued me when I passed out; the kind man who told me he tore up my check; the kind, and very handsome man.

No, I can't go there. Too soon.

# *Chapter Five*

Braydon was a little confused. The floral request was for a huge bouquet of pink roses to be delivered to a class room at Vista del Mar High School. Room 38. The salutation only said to deliver to Special Teacher. That was crazy, no name. The credit card that he ran through was in the name of D. Walker. Strange. He knew the latest principal was Bruce Walker, but who was the D.? Anyway, it was a valid card, so he put together the big bouquet of pastel roses. But, pink?

He knew they could denote appreciation, but they could also mean love and admiration. Braydon knew the speculative meaning behind every rose color, but this one mystified him. Why pink? Who, he wondered, was the teacher in Room 38?

He also wondered why the bouquet was ordered from his floral shop. So many people lately use the internet. Then, he remembered the order was to be delivered immediately. That was probably why, since even the internet orders took at least a day. Even with one day shipping. Plus, he could deliver in person, avoiding the UPS or FEDX delivery.

Who was the teacher in Room 38?

Braydon parked his floral delivery van in a slot near the school office. He had made the bouquet extra special with a wrapping of tulle. It appeared to float right out of his arms. The recipient would surely gasp at the loveliness when he presented it. It was truly eloquent, one of his best.

He was a little confused about how to deliver it. Should he just traipse to Room 38 and open the door? Or, should he be announced?

He decided to stop at the main receptionist's desk and sucked in his breath. What a surprise. Mrs. Beasley was still there!

"Well, my heavens to glory," she exclaimed. "Is that really you, Braydon?"

He nodded feeling heat creep up his neck and cheeks. She still remembered him after all those years? Was it because of the time he let out the former principal's tires, the time he mooned the P.E. coach, or the times he had finally grown up and led the debate team to victory? He hoped and prayed the latter.

"So," she said with a grin she was trying to contain. "Mr. Mooner." She chuckled then, just loud enough the others in the front office gave her questioning looks. "One of our former, exceptional students." She had emphasized the word exceptional.

Braydon wanted to melt into the tile floor, but with extreme effort he stood tall. "How nice to see you, Mrs. Beasley. So glad you are still here." He wanted to add, "in charge, and embarrassing former students." Instead, he grinned and plucked one rosebud from the arrangement and handed it to her with a bow. "For you."

"Oh, my! Thank you." Her smile illuminated her jowly cheeks. "Won't it be missed in the bouquet?"

"Probably not, since it's such a large bouquet, and," he added, "because the recipient isn't expecting it. So, I doubt if she will count the roses." He grinned. "Can you tell me where room 38 is?"

"Braydon," she whispered leaning over her desk toward him exposing a cleavage from her low-necked blouse. Was that appropriate attire for a school district employee? Especially, an almost ancient one with sagging skin? He almost shook his head to rid it of the unkind thought.

"I want you to know that I got such a kick out of you mooning Coach Wilson. He really deserved it." She plopped back in her swivel chair, snickered and sent him an air kiss with her fingertips.

Braydon reached across to clasp one of her hands, squeezed it gently and said, "You were always the best, Mrs. Beasley. Thank you." Did that comment redeem him?

"Now," she gestured, "Room 38 is down that hall and on your left. Just tap on the door, then open it quietly. Good luck."

Braydon remembered the smells of sweat of young athletes and overly used perfume by teen girls. The lingering odor of mac and cheese lunches and spilled Cokes. He lived in a whole different world now. But, it was fun to be back. For a few minutes.

He wandered down the corridor to Room 38. Most classroom doors were open, at least a little. When he approached his destination, he heard a voice he recognized.

"Wonderful students," it said melodically. "Let's get right down to Lady Macbeth. Let's analyze her." Papers shuffling, otherwise silence.

"Joshua, give us her profile. I know you told us you want to be a psychologist. So, you should have a good take on her."

Braydon had never had a teacher encourage students in this manner. Mrs. Dudley had been very encouraging, but more traditional in her approach, making each student memorize a scene and present it to the class. This was fun. He lingered outside the slightly open door for a few minutes to hear the rest of this unique teaching. Josh proceeded to describe Lady Macbeth with what Braydon thought was a lot of psychological mumbo jumbo. Bio polar, schizophrenia and especially obsessive compulsive disorder, OCD as he explained it. Josh was on a roll, and Noelle had to contain him. She eventually did with effusive thanks and compliments on his research.

Finally, he felt guilty eavesdropping and tapped lightly on the door frame. Beautiful Noelle looked toward him. She looked confused, but gestured him in with a wave of her hand.

He made an instant decision to make a grand entrance. For Noelle this should be special.

"For you." He bowed.

"Me? From you?"

"No, sorry. I believe it's a secret admirer."

He felt like a heel when he left the classroom. The students were hooting and whistling, and Noelle's face was crimson. Like his Candy Cane roses. Those are what she deserved, not pale pink.

Braydon raced back to his van in the school parking lot and slumped in his seat. If he had known the rose bouquet was for Noelle, he would have had one of his delivery guys take it. But, there had been no name on the delivery request, only Room 38. Because it was his old high school, he thought it would be fun to visit. Not so.

Too many memories, and now a new one. Would she believe he had nothing to do with the roses, except delivering them? Who was her secret admirer? How he would love to know.

When he got back to his shop, he decided to call the credit card company. He could do that as a proprietor. They could give him more information.

"What?" He put the phone down. He was more confused than ever. The name on the card was a woman's. Did a woman have a secret admiration for Noelle? Aw, there was another name on the card, the co- holder of the card. Bruce Walker, the recently new principal of Vista del Mar High School. Maybe Noelle was in love with him. Maybe that's why she cancelled her wedding. But then he remembered the yellow bruise on her wrist when she had looked at her watch the day she fainted. From Bruce, or from her former fiancé?

~

Noelle looked around in confusion. Mandy Smith who was longing to be a teacher's pet, jumped up. As she raced to the door, her blonde ponytail swinging like its namesake, she announced, "I will find a vase, a big vase, Ms. Day."

Noelle nodded mutely. She searched the enormous bouquet for a card, but found none. To be sure she stuck her hand down the middle of the roses and came up empty. They were glorious, such a delicate pale pink. Mandy raced back into the room holding a very large ordinary looking container.

"It's not exactly a vase, Ms. Day, but it's all Mrs. Beasley could come up with." The teen paused, then added. "They are so beautiful, it doesn't matter. Whatever you put them in, it will be dwarfed by their opulence." Mandy marched to her desk, straightened her too short skirt and slid gracefully into her seat.

Dwarfed? Opulence? Where did this child get those sophisticated words? Not from Shakespeare. Maybe she should start giving spelling tests again. But, to twelfth graders? She rubbed the side of her nose to ponder that thought. Well, why not? Sure, they all used spell check now on their laptops, but did they truly understand the meanings of the words? Maybe a spelling test with descriptive meanings. Not multiple choice.

Today was the last day before Winter Break (why couldn't the PCs call it by its proper name, Christmas Break?), so at least she wouldn't have to face all the teachers, staff and the insufferable principal for two weeks. By now, they all knew she had cancelled the wedding, or at least would know by tomorrow's mail when the un-announcement cards showed up.

Noelle had to pass through the front office to reach her car. Not only was she still burdened with her laptop, heavy purse and tote bag, but now with a container overflowing with pink roses. She knew there would be questions, and she dreaded them. Hopefully, Mrs. Beasley, The Busy Bee, as the teachers called her because she was into everyone's business, would be on a long phone conversation. No such luck.

Busy Bee waved her hand to stop Noelle, then hung up her phone. The woman couldn't resist prying. Noelle decided to jump ahead of her. "Thank you so much, Mrs. B. for giving my student a container for the flowers. That was very nice of you to help her out."

"Oh." Busy's hand went to her throat. "Least I could do. Glad I had one."

Noelle made a swift getaway. Waving her elbow because she had no free hand with all her luggage and the flowers, she cheerily called, "Have a blessed Christmas."

The older woman nodded. "You, too." But, her mouth formed an O, most likely to ask who the flowers were from. Noelle pretended not to notice and zoomed out the door pushing it with her shoulder so she wouldn't spill anything.

Whew! Made it! She popped open her trunk from the remote on her key fob and felt a hand on her shoulder. Startled, she swung around and found herself in the grasp of a big man's arms. Bruce Walker!

"**Mr.** Walker! Please let me go." She prayed her voice was strong enough to make the message clear. Very clear.

Instead of releasing her, he kept his arms lightly around her. "Did you like the flowers?"

Noelle had never reacted this way to anyone before, but without thinking, she spit in his face. OMGosh. Bruce Walker's face.

"I guess I deserved that." Her principal said.

She didn't reply; instead, rushed to her car door and jumped in turning the key in the ignition. Her hands trembled as she tried to maneuver the seat belt to click and backed out of her parking space without looking for cars on either side. She pressed the pedal to the metal (a common flip remark her students said), swung around almost missing Bruce Walker who jumped slightly off to the side. Looking back in the rear view mirror, she saw him standing with arms at his side and head bowed.

# *Chapter Six*

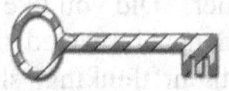

Noelle pulled into an empty parking spot at her condo and slammed the breaks so hard her little car rocked. She pushed the button on the door to pop the trunk open, took a deep breath, shimmied out of her seat and bee-lined to the rear of the BMW. This had not been a good day.

The last day before Winter Break was supposed to be uplifting, fun and hold promise. The only really good thing that had happened to her was the roses … until she learned who they were from. And, in the parking lot yet.

She tried to swallow the acrid taste in her mouth from her encounter with Bruce Walker. Had she really spit on him? In his face no less? So unlike her; she really wasn't all that brave, but maybe having the courage to break off with Clay … She shook her head to clear the nasty memories, both of

Clay and Bruce. He would probably write her up for the spitting incident. It would go on her permanent record and follow her everywhere for the rest of her career – to every school, every job she would ever interview for. Well, she didn't care. She couldn't care. Her self- worth was more important than a notation on a written piece of paper.

Rubbing her arm again, she hefted all her stuff from the trunk of her car and slammed it shut hard. She tromped to her condo door. All of her stuff, bags and purse and tote, hung from her left arm. Just as she was fumbling in her purse for her key to unlock the security screen door, she tripped on something. Something big.

What was the Christmas wreath she'd hung on the inner door doing on the entry floor? She checked the screen. It was still locked securely. But, how? Someone must have made a copy of her door key. Who would do such a thing?

Clay? But, she'd never given him one. Still, he could have sneaked it from her purse one time when they were in Home Depot and quickly had it copied. Surely, she would have noticed.

Braydon the floral guy would have had the opportunity when she'd collapsed in his arms at the hotel. But, he wouldn't have known much about her then, so why would he do that?

She inserted the key in the security door lock. It swung open easily. Looking back at the wreath on the floor of the cement stoop she shook her head. It was only a wreath, only a thing. Who placed it there she would figure out later. She was tired.

She kicked off her shoes and dropped all her

gear on the floor next to them. Padding into the kitchen she grabbed a bottle of icy water from the fridge and guzzled it. The dreaded answering machine was blinking, and the little window on the console displayed 3. Maybe Mom just wanting to chat was one, but who could the other two be?

Feeling a bit more centered in her bare feet and cooled by the cold water, she pressed the button. "You have three new messages." No kidding. I can read. Maybe she was still a bit irritated by the events of the day. Taking a deep breath, she grabbed a notepad and pen just in case there was a number she needed to write down. But, who on earth would call whose number she didn't know? Unless it was a sales pitch, and that she would delete.

"Hi, 'No'." Mom's cheery voice sang her nickname from the answering device. "Thinking last day of school maybe you want to come to dinner to celebrate? Dad made his infamous," chuckle, "chili. Tastes good to me, but he is never satisfied." Before Mom hung up, she said, "Let me know. Love to have you." Noelle heard a click, then the automated voice saying, "Message Number Two."

"No ... elle." He dragged her name out. His voice made her stomach churn, and she set down the almost empty bottle of water and clung to the side of the sink. She didn't want to hear what Clay said and had the presence of mind to click to the next message. Not much better.

"Noelle, sweet Noelle," Bruce Walker's deep voice sounded as if he was trying to be kind and sensitive. Not so. She wasn't sure which voice was more disgusting and upsetting, Clay's or Bruce's. Both were so phony.

She clicked off the machine, ignoring both messages, and called Mom to say she would love Dad's chili tonight. With lots of onions and cheese.

Mom hugged her tight. So did Dad. She needed that.

"So, tell me about your last day at school before break." Of course Mom was clueless. Should she share? Or, just say it was fine? She decided to be honest.

"Roses! How wonderful!"

"Not exactly, Mom. But, they were beautiful." She paused, maybe a bit dramatically. "Until I threw them in the trash."

Mom's blank expression sought Noelle's face.

Sipping her fizzy cranberry juice, Noelle explained about Bruce admitting to send them, and Braydon looking uncomfortable delivering them. And, Mrs. Beasley, Busy Bee, and her comments. The entire day tumbled out, including Mandy Smith rushing to secure a vase for the roses from Busy Bee. She decided not to share her spitting in Bruce's face, though. That was over the top.

"Sounds exciting, Noelle. But, stressful." Dad hadn't a clue how stressful. Men!

Mom put everything in order and in perspective. She rounded the coffee table and slid next to Noelle on the sofa. Hugging her daughter, she said, "So sorry. So very sorry."

They had intended to eat dinner in silence, but

the football game between two famous colleges was on TV, and Noelle insisted he watch it. She hadn't figured on volume up high, but, whatever. He had made the chili, and it was delicious. She added more onions.

Noelle stretched and snuggled into the covers loving the luxury of sleeping in. Saturday. No school, no obligations for two weeks. No students, no Bruce Walker.

She had turned off the phone ringer last night, but the annoying voice from the answering machine invaded her sleepiness. What?

"Noelle, are we still on for tonight, for dinner?" Bruce Walker's ingratiating voice sounded syrupy. She had never agreed to dinner tonight, nor any other, with that despicable man. No matter he was her boss. The very thought of him made her mouth dry and sour. She would delete the message. No way would she return it.

She threw off the luxurious covers and stumbled to the shower. The pounding needles of hot water felt so good, rinsing away voices in her head and on her answering machine.

Today she and Mom would go antiquing and maybe stop at a few garage sales. Just for fun. Mom was always looking for some special little thing. Noelle was looking for peace.

# *Chapter Seven*

"You would think the garage sales in Newport Beach would have great stuff," Mom said. Her voice sounded sneery and exasperated.

Noelle smiled. "Maybe we should have gone to the consignment stores and the thrift stores in Santa Ana. We always find something good in them."

She was about to lead Mom back to the car when she heard her name called. By a man. Turning abruptly, she saw the flower man, Braydon. What was he doing here?

Braydon rushed over to her. His arms were outstretched and a glowing smile spread across his handsome face. Noelle hadn't realized how good looking he was because she had only collapsed in his arms in the hotel lobby and caught just a quick look when he apologetically delivered the flowers to her class room. Well, also when he backed into her car.

Wow! Blonde hair that threatened to sneak down his forehead, intense blue eyes that twinkled in the early sunlight, and a chiseled jaw defined his face. She caught her breath. Did she really want to engage this man in conversation?

Yes, she did.

Noelle raised her hand in a slight off-hand greeting. He wasn't really an old friend, so she didn't want to be effusive. Braydon rushed over to her and placed his hand gently on her arm.

"How nice to see you again, Noelle. You look radiant." His smile beamed, and his blue eyes searched her face. They explored her eyes and remained there for a few seconds. Noelle shivered at his touch on her arm.

"Oh, it is cold this morning – finally, after such a hot summer." He laughed lightly and turned toward Mom. "And, who is this lovely lady with you?"

Noelle tried to compose herself, and remembering her manners, she gestured between Braydon and Mom and introduced them.

"Mom, this is Braydon Lovejoy who rescued me when I passed out in the hotel lobby. He owns the Love In Bloom flower shop in Corona del Mar." She hesitated, but pressed on. "He is the florist who was going to provide the Calla Lilies for … well, you know what."

~

Braydon worried about Noelle's reaction to his touch. She had shirked back immediately and rubbed her arm. He remembered the yellow bruise he'd seen on her wrist when she had passed out in the hotel lobby and he had lifted her onto the sofa there. Had someone abused her? If so, why had she allowed it?

He didn't know much about abuse, but he had read a bit about it on the internet. Still, was he making an assumption? He hoped and prayed he was wrong. Noclle was a lovely girl, and from everything he knew about her she deserved respect. At least that. He couldn't imagine anyone hurting her physically. But, how did she get that yellow mark on her wrist?

~

"What's the matter?" Mom looked at her quizzically when they'd settled back in the rental car. Her red "baby" was in the body shop, the one that specialized in fancy foreign cars. At least it would be repaired by the end of school break.

"Oh, nothing. Not much, anyway." Noelle felt very confused. What was it about Braydon that affected her? She was sure her heart was visibly pounding at the front of her tee shirt. And her hands shook on the steering wheel of the unfamiliar car. She hoped Mom wouldn't notice.

"You like him?" The question hung in the air between them as Noelle started the car. "He seems like such a gentleman. Handsome, too. But," she paused, "things and people aren't always what they seem."

"That I know. From experience."

"Sadly, yes."

"Let's ditch the garage sales and run into the thrift shops in Santa Ana. K?"

Mom nodded and gave a thumbs up. "Maybe we'll see something special, something we can't resist."

They spent a few hours traipsing from The Goodwill to The Salvation Army to the Saint Vincent de Paul shops. Nothing struck their fancy, but they had fun just being together – something they hadn't gotten to do often when Noelle was engaged and making wedding plans.

Exiting the freeway at MacArthur Boulevard they realized they were starving and decided to stop for lunch at Tommy Bahama's, one of their favorites, and eat outside on the patio. The salads were outstanding, and the patio was shaded by big umbrellas and warmed by heaters. With both their mouths watering they parked and jostled in line. Because there were only two of them, they were seated almost immediately while parties of four or more had to wait. They settled back in chairs under a heated umbrella.

"This is so nice." Mom spread the thick cotton napkin on her lap.

"I agree. I especially love that although it's busy, every table seems private and secluded."

A jaunty server appeared to take their orders. Blue crab salad, their favorite.

"Would you like to start with a cup of soup?" he asked. "The crab bisque is divine. I know it's a lot of crab, but both are so delicious." He smiled and waited patiently for the women to decide.

They both loved seafood, especially crab, so they acquiesced. Noelle sighed, relishing in her time with Mom and her freedom from control. How, she wondered, had she ever succumbed to that? She had been raised a strong, independent woman by wonderful, loving parents. Had she been so desperate for the love of a man that she had almost given up her soul?

The two women sipped their raspberry iced tea in frosty glasses. The ambiance was perfect. Other diners chatted quietly. They were undisturbed. Until ...

A shrill voice interrupted their reverie, and an imposing form hovered over them casting a shadow.

"Kerstin, Noelle, *so* nice to see you." The syrupy voice dripped. Clay's mother, Gladys, placed a hand on Noelle's shoulder. Noelle shirked back and let out a gurgled cry.

"What's wrong, dear?" She emphasized the word dear. "You having regrets about the breakup, Miss Fickle? Maybe you have second thoughts about what you let go."

Noelle wanted to gag. She held her napkin up to her mouth and started to push back her chair. Kerstin slipped her hand under the tablecloth and squeezed Noelle's knee while barely shaking her head. She didn't think the other woman even noticed, she was so focused on being mean and derogatory. Gladys droned on about how Clay was moving forward happily – new job, new girlfriend – happy man. She gestured a lot, always had, and the diamond and precious stone bracelets on her wrists jingled together.

"Oh, you probably know his new love. I think you either went to high school together, or she may be a teacher at Vista del Mar."

Noelle looked at her curiously after making a play of patting her lips with the napkin she'd almost choked into. Her first thought was *That was fast.* Her second was *Poor girl.* She wasn't sure she wanted to know the "new love's" name, but if she did, she could at least pray for her. She would need it, lots of prayer.

As Gladys whined on, she realized the woman was dying to tell her the name. Of course, she couldn't resist.

"Surely, you must know her. Melanie Carson. Her mother is married to the principal."

Noelle coughed to abate almost gagging again. So, that letch was stepfather to a woman her age. That meant Bruce Walker was almost her parents' ages. How disgusting.

She desperately wanted to leave the table for the restroom, but she didn't want to leave Mom alone to deal with this horrible woman. How had she ever thought she could accept her lovingly as a mother-in-law?

Just then Mom raised her hand in greeting to someone behind Noelle. She winked quickly at Noelle and rose with an "Excuse me. See a friend."

Gladys didn't bat an eye, just kept telling Noelle about Clay's wonderful new job – traveling salesman for a noted pharmaceutical company. Like Noelle cared. She did have a fleeting thought, though, about how accessible drugs would be to him.

Mom had been gone a few minutes. Where was she? Suddenly, she heard soft laughter behind her. Mom's voice and a male's.

Kerstin rounded the table with her hand tucked into Braydon's elbow. What?

"Braydon asked if he might join us, dear. Wasn't that sweet of him?" Kerstin's smile was a tad devilish, and Braydon bent toward Noelle's cheek to give it a peck.

"Oh!" Noelle was sure she blushed. Maybe that was a good thing in this circumstance. She had to hold in a giggle when she realized Gladys was finally winding down.

"I see you've moved on, too." The obnoxious woman slitted her eyes and peered boldly at Braydon. "Who is this?"

"This is my friend Braydon Lovejoy." Noelle had finally found her voice, and was she having fun! "He owns Love In Bloom Floral Shop in Corona del Mar."

Braydon stepped forward and took Gladys' hand planting a lip-touch on its back. "So very pleased to meet you, Madam." He smiled that wonderful smile that lit up his face. "I believe it was you who requested Calla Lilies for Noelle's former" he paused very briefly, "event."

Gladys nodded, her face chalk white, just like the lilies she had wanted Noelle to carry as a bride. "Yes," she whispered. "Me."

"I still have them on order from a purveyor in Central America. If you still want them for any other special occasion, please let me know. They are quite expensive, but I am sure that is not an issue with you."

He bowed slightly and reached over to pull out the chair Gladys was standing behind. "May I escort you to your table?"

"No, thanks. My friends are waiting for me. Nice to meetcha," she slurred. Had she had too much pre-lunch wine, or was she just upset? Noelle, Kerstin and Braydon watched her march off into the inside dining area. Maybe she did have friends waiting for her, or maybe she didn't.

# *Chapter Eight*

Before the three had a chance to look at each other, the server appeared with three cups of bisque. He looked at Braydon. "I hope I did the right thing, Sir. You always order it."

"Yes, perfect. Thank you, Kevin." He paused. "I'll have whatever the ladies are having."

"Certainly, Sir. They are also having your favorite salad." The server turned away with a grin and an over the shoulder thumbs up.

The three of them laughed. It felt so good. But, Noelle had to know.

"What happened here? I mean how did this happen?"

Kerstin went first. "I was praying desperately for a way to get out of the Gladys situation. Then, I saw Braydon. I sensed he is a kind man and an understanding one. Maybe a Christian, too?" She looked toward Braydon, and he nodded enthusiastically. "Since we had met this morning at a random garage sale ... well, you know I believe in God's divine intervention." She paused to place a hand on her throat. To suppress a giggle? "I just went for it, as you young people say."

Braydon reached to clasp both of their hands. His grin challenged the Cheshire Cat. He was obviously happy.

"Kerstin, may I call you that?" He squeezed her fingers lightly and she had her turn to grin. "You gave me the perfect opening to ask Noelle for a date. But, more than that, you trusted me. Thank you for that."

Noelle saw Mom's eyes fill with moisture.

"I will never betray your trust. Not in me as a man, nor as a friend to Noelle and you. I promise."

Noelle blinked back tears. This was a special man. Not a man who would deceive her or hurt her. Dabbing her eyes with her napkin, she rested her hands on her lap. Still, curiosity overcame her. Must be the teacher in her.

"Now," Noelle said, "I want to find out how this all happened. Like, where did you get your courage, Mom, your inspiration? And, Braydon, what did Mom say to you to convince you to participate in this fiasco? And, how does the waiter know you and what you eat?" So many questions. She wanted answers.

"What I said ..." She nodded to have Braydon take over. She had gone beyond her limits to silence Gladys. Then, Braydon appeared out of the blue, and she jumped on the opportunity without thinking. Just reacting.

"Your mother," he turned to smile at Kerstin, "was brave. And, she trusted the Lord, and me. Thank you, Kerstin."

Her head bowed. "Yes, I did get very brave. I had only met Braydon this morning, but I had a sense about him. Not only could he be trusted, but he and you," she turned to Noelle, "had electricity between you." She looked her daughter in the eyes. "I saw your hands shaking as we were driving away after you saw Braydon. I knew in my heart there was a connection between you. Maybe the 'right' one, the one I've been praying for."

"Mom!" Noelle was mortified that her mother was so blunt. "Puh-leese. You're embarrassing me. My hands were shaking because of the rental car, not being used to driving it."

"Oh, shush. I saw the way you two looked at each other." Kerstin waved a dismissive hand in the air.

Noelle felt heat rush to her cheeks. Sometimes Mom could be so direct. Usually, she liked the fact that Mom held no punches, told things the way she saw them, and was super honest. But, why now? She composed herself, but before digging into her luscious looking soup pressed on.

"But, Mom," she glared pointedly at Kerstin, "what did you say to Braydon to make him come to our table and act so conciliatory? I know he's a gentleman, but you must have coerced him to portray 'friend.'"

"Well," she said, head held high this time. "I

took charge. Away from that despicable Gladys.

When I noticed Braydon coming into the patio, I ran up to him and reintroduced myself. He didn't need a reminder. I told him who Gladys was, briefly whose mother she is, and I needed help. When he saw it was you being badgered by her, he immediately took action. Gentlemanliness took over." Her smile toward Braydon glowed. "Thank you."

Braydon grabbed Noelle's hand and laughed heartily. He gave it a squeeze, then reached for Kerstin's hand. "I am sorry you both had to go through so much drama, but I am very glad I was here to partake in the fun." He hesitated. All their crab salads had just been placed before them.

"Do you mind if I pray?"

Both women nodded agreement and closed their eyes.

"Dear Heavenly Father, thank you for this delightful and nourishing food. Thank you, too, for new friendships. We ask for Your blessing on all. Amen."

# *Chapter Nine*

Braydon insisted on paying for all three lunches. "It is really my pleasure. And, thank you for including me in the fun." He turned toward Kerstin. "And, for trusting me."

"I have a sense about people." She winked. "It was easy to trust you."

He winked back and touched her hand. "Thank you. I hope Noelle does, too." Turning to the younger woman, he looked her directly in the face. "I hope you will have lunch with me tomorrow afternoon?"

"Oh, really?" She looked toward her mother who nodded slightly. "Yes. Thank you. I'd love to. Where can I meet you?"

"How about Mayur? Do you like Indian food?"

"I adore it, and Mayur. What time?"

"Is one okay?"

"Perfect." He hesitated. "I am happy to pick you up, but I sense you will be more comfortable meeting me there?" She nodded.

"Great. Wear comfy shoes because I thought it might be fun to either walk above Big Corona Beach on Fifth Avenue, or maybe explore the Sherman Foundation Gardens. That okay with you?"

"Sure. Either one. But, why the Gardens?"

He hesitated. "Because I am a volunteer board member there." Noticing Noelle's quizzical look, he explained. "I specialize in roses, one of the few board members who does."

Noelle had been to Sherman Gardens many times for events. The Vista del Mar PTA had an annual fund-raising home tour that included lunch at the Gardens. It was a lovely diversion from the classroom, and the PTA sponsored so many things for the school and teachers. It was also a venue for weddings and special events like bridal showers, including her own. Could she do this without an ache on her soul?

They parted, and she and Mom went to Bristol Farms to find something yummy for dinner. Daddy was away for the weekend doing one of his special weight loss lectures in New Mexico. The evening would be a girls' night, maybe re-watching one of her favorite movies, either Flashdance or Dirty Dancing. Both had such good messages, and she often hummed the music from each. Tonight would be fun!

Noelle parked her beige rental car in the side parking lot and adjusted the laces on her Converse shoes. Normally, she wouldn't wear such casual attire to a restaurant for a date. But, was this a real date? Braydon had insisted, politely, on comfy walking shoes. Fortunately, California, and Corona del Mar in particular, was dress casual. Maybe if, someday, they went to the Five Crowns, she would dress up more.

She felt as if she really did trust Braydon. And, Mom trusted him. Noelle sensed Mom had never really trusted Clay, always had reservations, but never spoke them. She had often noticed worry lines around Mom's eyes when she talked about him. She was the kind of mother who didn't pry, but prayed.

Maybe it was time to show Mom her yellow bruises.

Braydon rushed down to the parking lot to take her hand. He had gotten a great spot right in front of the restaurant. "I wanted to save it for you, but I knew the minute I gave it up, it would be gone."

"That's okay. Better to leave my car here to come back to after our walk."

"You still want to do that?"

"Sure. Let's see how we feel after we eat. After my order of Lamb Sag," she teased.

~

His order of Tandori Chicken and hers of Lamb Sag were delicious. Braydon managed to get a table at the window looking out on the sidewalk where they could watch all the "beautiful people" and the "funny people" sauntering by with dogs, or just holding hands. It was a plethora of interesting, sometimes strange, people. Most were laughing. Good sign.

Noelle fiddled with the last bites of her lamb. They had had a lot of fun joking about the people walking outside the window. Light conversation suited her fine.

So, why was she scared?

Braydon reached across the small table and touched her hand, the one that still had her fork in it. "Are you up to a short walk?"

"I think so. I am really curious about your involvement in Sherman Gardens. Are we going there?"

"If you don't mind?" He paid the bill and offered his hand to Noelle. "Let's take my car so we don't have to walk so far."

She accepted, still a little worried. She hadn't even really dated in two years, and certainly not after her breakup with Clay. Climbing into his car she started to shake. That was the first place Clay had grabbed her arm and twisted it and left marks. *What am I doing here, Lord?*

Braydon reached across the console and laid his hand gently on her forearm. For some crazy reason it calmed her to be touched by him, but not be grabbed so tight it hurt. His touch was gentle, even though she felt it through her sleeve on one of the yellow bruises. She avoided rubbing it so he wouldn't notice and question her action.

He pulled into the Sherman Foundation's parking lot. "Whew, looks busy today. Must be some kind of event. Of course it is Sunday." Offering his arm to ascend the steps, she accepted and bravely tucked her fingers into its crook.

Noelle had been so nervous the day of her wedding shower that she had barely looked around and taken in the beauty of the gardens and its fountains and ponds. The other five Candy Canes had hustled her into the restaurant where she was immediately the center of attention and introduced to at least fifty women she didn't know – Gladys' cronies. The woman either belonged to or sat on the board of numerous societies. Of course she had invited almost everyone she knew, all simpering and chatty. Mom had been more selective, just inviting close friends and neighbors and women from her Bible study and garden club. People she cared about. She told Noelle later she was sure Gladys was vying for more gifts. Now, Noelle had to tackle the huge trial of returning over eighty shower gifts and even more wedding ones. She had planned to do it during Winter Break. Instead, she was spending more quality time with Mom, and now with Braydon. Still, she mustn't put it off. That would be rude and give Gladys more ammunition to say ugly things about her and spread rumors. She shoved the thought aside as Braydon guided her past a beautiful pond that he explained was the focal point of the Central Garden.

Several ladies in blue smocks waved to Braydon as they strolled down a long brick path. Braydon smiled widely, and Noelle sniffed the air dramatically. "Follow the scent," he quipped.

"Heavenly." They stopped next to a compact

garden, much smaller than some of the others with native plants. Probably large succulents and cacti took up more space. "Oh, Braydon, this is exquisite. All those gorgeous colors!"

"Twenty-seven varieties." He sounded so proud. "Maybe not exactly twenty-seven colors, but close." He pointed to a bush with huge blooms of deep red. "That's a unique one called Splash of Red. The Garden is blessed to have it."

"It's lovely. They all are." She shaded her forehead with a hand. The late afternoon sun was playing havoc with her eyes, and she had forgotten to wear her sunglasses. "I'm sure Mom has seen the gardens many times over the years, but she adores roses and needs to see these again soon. Maybe her garden club could take a tour."

"Absolutely. There are numerous tours, including some for students. She just missed the rose pruning demonstration, though." He pulled her away from the roses. "It's about time for the garden to close, but let's go find a brochure that lists all the events and tours."

She settled in the passenger seat of his little Mercedes and glanced through the brochure they'd picked up. "You mentioned student tours, but I don't see any listed here."

"I think you have to specifically arrange for them and even pay for bus transportation."

"I don't see a problem with that part, the paying for buses part. Our wonderful PTA gives each teacher a stipend to use as we see fit, as long as it complements our subject." She giggled. "I heard that last year one of the math teachers took her students to the dog surfing contest in Huntington Beach. Of course the kids loved it. I'm sure she figured out how to make math a major part of the outing.

"Maybe I could do that with English. Of course, right now we are studying the Bard, not Gertrude Stein." Braydon snickered at that comment.

# *Chapter Ten*

She pulled out the butterfly decorated notecards and handed a stack to each Candy Cane. Her dear friends had gathered to help her write the thank yous, actually the *no* thank yous. It was an arduous task, but at least none of the formerly invited wedding guests or women who had attended the shower knew her handwriting. Just a bit of deception.

Being an organized person she gave each girl a separate list of addresses and names and what the gift had been. About fifty plus each. What dear friends they were to help with this daunting undertaking. Fortunately, they loved being together, and they loved pizza.

Noelle laughed after she'd tipped the pizza delivery boy, or was it a girl? Sometimes hard to tell nowadays. Whoever it was had both arms embellished with flamboyant tattoos. She wondered how that person would feel about those when he or she turned seventy. Surely, they would be wrinkled and even faded. Would the kids they have in their earlier years question?

She laid the two boxes on the kitchen table with paper plates and forks and knives and a grouping of soft drinks. Fortunately, napkins were included with the delivery. She had already made a huge green salad, knowing as much as they all loved pizza, salad was a must for keeping a slim waistline.

"Gosh, Noelle, you even gave us the words to say." Cindy grinned at her. "I love it! Don't have to be creative."

Noelle had printed out a generic, sort of all-purpose message for each girl to write on each notecard. All five girls had it propped in front of them in plastic "proppers," as Noelle dubbed them. Picked up at Office Max and Staples. She wanted to make this task as easy as possible for them. They were such wonderful friends to donate their time, and to be stuck with crimson bridesmaid gowns they will probably never wear. Maybe Connie who was a designer for a large corporate firm could wear it to a fancy function. But, Natalie owned her own small health gym and probably would have no use for it in the future. Unless, Connie invited her. Now, there's a possibility.

Noelle's heart filled with guilt. Not one of them had complained about paying for attendant gowns that now hung limply in their closets. Even Candy who was back home living with her parents after a difficult divorce. The only one who accepted it so graciously without batting an eye was Doreen. Noelle wasn't totally certain about her circumstances. She was the more private one, the one who didn't share much. Still, she was here and laughing with the other girls.

Noelle chuckled under her breath. The Three Cs, the Two Ns and the D. That had almost become a moniker, in addition to the Candy Canes one.

"Okay, girls, ladies, whatever you prefer to be called now that we are all *so* old ..." She lifted a spoon and clanged it against a Pepsi can. "Let's go in order. Candy first." They had used to do that when deciding whom should swim first in the relays. Of course, it was really up to coach Douglas, but it almost always worked out. "Pick your pizza, girl."

Everyone laughed remembering the years of fun they'd had in high school. Even teasing Coach Douglas until he relented letting them chose their spots in each relay. "You know your times and abilities," he'd said. "I trust you." He was right. They won almost every time.

Candy filled her plate with salad and one slim piece of pizza. Noelle frowned. The girl was too skinny already.

"Next, Cindy and Connie. Go, girls." She hoped to make this fun and bring back memories. Good ones.

"Natalie is next, then moi." She winked. Poor Doreen was always last because her last name started with a Z.

Doreen rose and sauntered to the table. "Yum! I

get everything that's left. So, don't expect any leftovers." She snickered. Noelle knew she was kidding. Doreen was the most generous of all of them.

The girls all finally rinsed their sauce laden hands under the kitchen faucet and got back to work. Noelle had also printed out all the envelopes in a script font on her computer. The only thing that worried her was to be sure each person's note coordinated with the right address. She would go through them all tomorrow and check, then take them to the Post Office and mail them. An agonizing ordeal, but when she did it, it would be final.

~

"Oh, dear," the petite older lady behind the counter, said. "You have a lot of envelopes." She smiled and bumbled with the huge stack. Then, they all collapsed and scattered over the floor behind the counter.

Noelle always tried to patronize the local Hallmark Store Post Office. She seldom had to stand in line there, and the clerks were so friendly. She also wanted to be sure it survived all the cuts the Post Office had threatened, like no delivery on Saturdays. She could have just dumped the one hundred and fifty or so envelopes in a local mail box, but she preferred to see them actually placed in the bin behind a P.O. counter. Was she too compulsive, too attentive to detail as Clay had blamed her for many times? Was that a fault? Or, did it perhaps make her a better teacher?

She shook her head and reached for the little

old strawberry-haired lady's hand. "Can I help? If I am allowed to come behind the counter, I really want to help." She wasn't sure how "official" this little Post Office was. But, she felt responsible for the flying envelopes disaster.

"No, no, dear. It's all right," she replied as her tiny body bent in a pretzel shape to retrieve the errant envelopes.

"What is going on here?" The imposing voice came from a tall, large-boned woman, also in her senior years, with a thick, long blonde braid down her back. "How did this happen, Maven? Why weren't these brought in a sack?" She turned and glared at Noelle.

"I am so sorry. I should have had them in a container and put them in the box in the parking lot. I prefer to mail inside an actual Post Office," Noelle explained. "My fault." She scanned the blonde's face, then her own broke into recognition.

"Mrs. Dudley! Is it really you?"

The woman squinted her eyes and stepped closer to the counter between her and Noelle. "And, you are?"

"I am Noelle Day. You were my junior English teacher." She paused, hoping a memory would resurface. "It's because of you that I am now an English teacher." She smiled, praying the woman hadn't lost her faculties. "You told me if I ever learned to spell, I could maybe be a good writer someday."

Suddenly, the woman's face lit up. "I remember. You were the one who liked to recite Shakespeare. Lady Macbeth, right?" She looked at

Noelle again. "You had two ponytails, one on either side."

Noelle nodded.

"My goodness. You have grown up."

Noelle nodded again, and this time found her voice. "I'm teaching at Vista del Mar. Senior English," she added. She pulled a business card out of her wallet. She wasn't sure why she'd even had some made. Seemed pretentious. Maybe this was the why.

# *Chapter Eleven*

Mrs. Dudley squinted. She even turned the card over. Then she smiled widely. "What a clever idea!"

"Not sure why I did it. Having cards printed." Noelle felt herself blushing. "I guess it was a bit presumptuous."

"No. Not at all." She turned the card over again. "You did become a good speller. Even won the Bee at your level." The older woman smiled at her again. "Perhaps editing was in your future, even then." She tucked the card into her smock pocket. "I will be sure to recommend you." She looked at Noelle kind of funny. "You have many clients?"

Noelle felt herself blush even more. "No, not too many. But, I don't have much time to devote to editing." She hoped she wouldn't have to list her few clients to the woman who now seemed so enthusiastic about her endeavor as a writing coach and editor. Still, she had been paid, even though a pittance, for editing Mom's garden club's brochure and Dad's business card. Hopefully, she could expand her business. It wasn't for the money, but it was something she loved doing.

"Well, you should pursue it. Might be a nice sideline for you during the summer." She looked at Noelle quizzically. "Unless you are teaching summer school?"

"Unfortunately," Noelle replied, "there is no optional summer school, like when I was a kid. Especially not for English."

Mrs. D. squinted. "That is way too bad. Financial cuts?"

"Yes, and a lack of interest in parents."

"I remember you and your friends used to ride your bikes to VDM to attend summer school in your red striped bathing suits so you could practice your strokes after class. Kept you, and them, out of trouble in those days." She rubbed a hand across her forehead looking troubled. "You still on swim team?" she asked.

Noelle wasn't sure how to reply. High school swim team had been over years ago. Was her old teacher in La La Land? She was embarrassed for her.

"Oops. Lost my train of thought. Guess I *am* getting old." Mrs. Dudley gave a self-deprecating chuckle. "Happens sometimes when I am having good memories." She shyly looked at Noelle. "I do know the Candy Canes and their fame was a long time ago. Sad no other team has followed yours."

"I am so glad your memories are good ones, Mrs. Dudley. Mine are, too."

Noelle and Mrs. Dudley finally had the courage to walk to the end of the little Post Office counter and hug. The little strawberry-colored hair employee nodded her approval as she sorted Noelle's envelopes into zip code piles.

~

The phone was ringing when she got home. Braydon? Hopefully. She picked it up hastily, and blurted out, "Hi!" She hadn't even looked at the caller I.D. What a fool.

"Hi to you, too." He'd had to assume she had looked at the little window and knew it was him. Whew!

"How about dinner tonight? My shop closes at five on Mondays." He rambled on before she could get a word in. "I thought it might be fun to eat in Fashion Island and see all the decorations. Have you seen the Bloomingdale tree yet?" Finally, he stopped for a breath.

She couldn't contain her laughter. "What's so funny?" He sounded a bit offended.

"You are. You didn't give me a chance to say one word."

"Oh, sorry. Well, can you?"

She heard him fussing with something. Maybe tissue paper or cellophane, wrappings for flowers. "What's that noise I hear? Sounds like you're crushing something."

"I am. Cleaning up and tossing used cellophane and wet tissue. Closing up shop."

"Oh, thought so."

"Well, can you?" She could tell he was trying to be patient, but she was having so much fun bantering with him. "Mmm. Maybe." She drew the word out dramatically.

"What's wrong? You don't want to go out with a florist?" Now, he did sound offended.

"Of course not. I love men who devote their lives to flowers." She couldn't help teasing him.

"Well, in case you're worried, I'm not 'that' way. I am a business owner, proprietor. Nothing swishy about me." Now, he sounded defensive. He probably got a lot of funny looks, even snide comments, when he mentioned he is a florist.

"Braydon, I know that." She paused for effect. "I never really thought that. Honest. I was fooling with you." She switched the phone to the other ear. "I just couldn't resist teasing."

"I would love to go to dinner tonight. I haven't had time to go to Fashion Island in ages. Too tired after teaching all day and ... dealing with former event planning. Besides, I need to buy a Christmas gift for Mom and Dad. Do you mind if we do a little shopping, too?"

She held her breath. Men seldom liked to shop, especially for people they didn't know well, like a girlfriend's parents. Oops. Was she a GF? Certainly not yet. Maybe ... someday.

"Actually, I don't mind at all. I just want to spend time with you." He sounded honest. "And, even though I haven't met your dad, I already adore your mother. Got any ideas?"

"That's so nice of you. No, I don't have any ideas at all, not a clue." She screwed up her face and wrinkled her nose. What could she buy for them? "What are you buying your mom? And, dad? You haven't mentioned him." She hoped she wasn't making a faux pas. What if Braydon's dad was deceased, or his parents were divorced. *Agh, Noelle, you big fumble bum.*

She could hear him laughing and slapping something. His knee? What had she done?

~

He got a kick out of Noelle's shaking voice when she apologized for asking about his dad. Dad would get a kick out of it, too, when he met Noelle. Hopefully, soon.

They agreed to meet at Bloomie's in the perfume department and try to do their shopping first before a relaxing dinner. When he arrived, Noelle was opening bottles and sniffing and spraying tester scents on her wrists. She looked up at him and smiled.

"I can never decide. Most smell so good, even delightful. But, some, ugh! I guess I prefer the old school, original ones. The ones bearing the famous women's names all smell yucky to me. I like fresh."

He leaned forward and placed a quick kiss on her cheek. She was fresh. Fresh and lovely. No pretense about her. How, he wondered, could any man abuse her? Still, he wasn't certain that had happened. He needed to get her to open up, share. Maybe she would do that tonight.

"I agree. The only heady scents I like are from roses. And maybe hyacinths and a few other flowers that are seldom sold in bouquets. But, for perfumes, I like soft, not clinging; sea breeze, not sexy."

She grinned and pushed a decorative glass perfume container toward him. "What do you think of this?"

"Mmm. Very nice. Light and fresh. Like your mother." He grinned back. "You thinking of getting that for her?"

"I am. Dad buys her the perfume she told him she liked about twenty years ago. It's nice. But, I think it's time for a new fragrance for her. From her daughter."

She bought a small spritzer size, just right for a purse. Of course Bloomie's wrapped it.

~

"Now," she said, "for Dad." She led him up to the second floor men's department. She knew he hated clothing with designer labels on them, so she avoided golf shirts. Dad likes simple things. But, he still had to wear a tie about three times a year when he was giving a presentation. She had always been drawn to the unique ties, but Dad was so conservative, so she hesitated. She finally found one in subdued grays, no designer label. She had it wrapped, such a luxury.

"What about your parents? Do you want to shop for them?"

"No. We do a kind of different thing."

"What do you do?"

"We donate to favorite charities that, of course, the recipient loves."

"How special. Have you done that for years? When did you decide? How much?"

"We have a fifty dollar limit. Doesn't seem like much, but it makes sense." He smiled and winked.

"I like that. But, don't you give even a little tree gift so you'd have something to open Christmas morning?"

"Of course we do. Couldn't resist that. Sometimes it's a Starbucks gift card, not very original, but definitely appreciated, especially by my lazy brother, Rob, who hates to make his own coffee." A deep chuckle from his throat startled her. "One year we all seemed to get the same idea." He paused, maybe for effect. "We had this precious little dog, Jake, who barfed a lot on the carpet and had constant accidents." He must have noticed the anxiety and frown wrinkling her brow. "Don't worry. Jake is in doggy heaven now. He had a seizure when he was eighteen. Dad rushed him to the vet's where he died. Peacefully," he added.

"So, what did you do in honor of Jake?"

"That year, we all seemed to have the same idea." he repeated. He cocked his head to be sure she was okay with what he was going to say. It was a bit off the wall.

"So, tell me." She looked askance at him.

"We all bought carpet cleaner!" He laughed. Did she get it?

"Actually, Dad got Mom a gift certificate for a carpet cleaning company to come in and do the job right."

Noelle burst into laughter. Holding her tummy, she said, "That is classic! That must have been fun, and," she concluded, "a tribute to Jake. Sort of."

Braydon propped his feet on the coffee table. What a fun and unusual evening with Noelle. He nursed his Starbucks latte, sipping it slowly. Pondering her responses to his family's unusual Christmas gifts, he felt pleased. Maybe she picked up on the idea for her own family.

He wanted to call her, but it was after ten.

# Chapter Twelve

Noelle was stewing. She slammed her door shut and locked it, the security lock, too. She had rehung the wreath on the inside door and decided not to worry about how it had fallen off. Clay's mother had said he had "moved on," and she didn't think he would bother her anymore. Maybe in her haste to leave the other morning with arms encumbered, it had slipped off its hook, and she hadn't noticed. So, it might have been her fault.

Taking off the plaid wool neck scarf she'd worn, since the weather had finally turned cooler, she hung it on a peg next to the closet door. She petitioned her Savior.

*What should I do, Lord? I am confused, especially since meeting Braydon so soon after my breakup with Clay. I know ... I know, he is a kind, obviously Christian, man. He has never done anything to offend me. Nor frighten me. Mom trusts him, too. That's a biggie.*

Even though it was late, she made a cup of coffee and plunked her legs on the coffee table. She wondered what Braydon was doing now. Did he feel the same way? Confused? They had only had two dates, if one could call lunch and a brief shopping trip to Fashion Island dates. Well, there was the unfortunate accident with his delivery van backing into her red, shiny new BMW baby. But, accidents do happen. And, sometimes, God provides them to bring people together. Still, she wondered if things weren't going too fast. Maybe she should call a respite.

*Yes, that's what I will do.*

~

Braydon checked his emails and was shocked.

He didn't understand the one from Noelle. What had he done to frighten her? He read it again.

Braydon,

You have been such a wonderful friend these few days. I am truly grateful. But, I feel as if our friendship is moving too fast. For me, at least. I hope you understand. I want to take a respite for a month, to see if we are still attracted to each other and still value our friendship. Everything happened so soon, maybe too soon for me. Please do not contact me for at least a month. I trust you in this. Thank you. Noelle.

He moved his computer mouse again to re-read

her post and to be sure. Then he cried.

~

Noelle's hand shook as she sent the email to Braydon. Did she do the right thing? She wasn't sure, but she sensed she had. She really cared for him. He had become such a good friend. Never pressuring her in any way. She felt her forehead where he had placed a light kiss. The kiss that had sent tingles up her spine. Now, just weeks before Christmas, she would be alone, again. She would have Mom and Dad, of course. But, no love in her life.

~

What did she mean by "contact?" Did she mean email, phone, personal? What if?

~

Noelle almost tripped over the bundle on her doorstep. She was headed to the gym, a treat she hadn't taken advantage of for weeks. The bundle was wrapped in what looked like the green stuff florists encased big bouquets in. She picked it up and found a small card attached to it.

*Dear Noelle,*

*I respect your asking me to not contact you personally. I hope this bouquet does not offend you. I really want you to have it.*

*Sent in friendship.*

*Braydon*

Noelle unwrapped the lovely bouquet of roses. She had mixed feelings. Yes, she had asked Braydon to honor a month's respite, but was this different? She wasn't sure as she found a large vase to accommodate the bouquet.

She sped to the gym and did the stair stepper and several other machines. After using free weights, she felt toned and worked out. She had forgotten about the opulent bouquet until she found a paper hanging out of her mailbox.

A poem.

Did he go overboard? He realized he had been a bit ambivalent. He had just gone with his gut feeling, and prayers. Maybe the poem was over the top. Maybe the roses were, too. Maybe he needed more discernment.

He set his iPhone calendar for four weeks. Could he wait that long? For her sake, for their sake, he would.

He shifted his feet on the coffee table, uncrossed his ankles. He was thinking about why that low table was called a coffee table. Must have been one of those anomalies from another century. The phone rang. The land line. Not used to hearing it, he rushed to pick it up.

"Braydon?" the soft voice said his name.

"Yes. And, you are?"

"So sorry. It's Noelle's mom, Kerstin. I guess I'm a little nervous." She drew in a breath. "Am I calling too late?"

"No, not at all. What can I do for you?" He hoped it had nothing to do with Noelle deciding on the month long respite.

"This is a bit spur of the moment, but I am hoping you can do it. I know you have a business to run, so I will understand if you can't." She blabbered on, and Braydon hoped she would get to the point soon. He really liked Kerstin, but he was tired and wanted to keep this conversation short.

"It's just a brief one hour presentation. I forgot I'm the member in charge this month to invite someone for that." She finally exhaled to Braydon's relief. He was afraid she might pass out. "Can you, could you possibly, do it?"

He pulled up his calendar again. "Tell me the date and time, Kerstin." He waited while he heard papers shuffling.

"This Wednesday morning at ten. Coffee and sweet rolls served, of course. Can you do it?"

"I will be happy to." He heard a huge sigh of relief. "What do you want me to talk about? What can I bring?"

"I dunno. Maybe roses? Since that is your expertise." Kirsten paused and he heard another rustling of papers. "I am looking over the member list. Preferences. Seems like most like to grow roses, but most of us aren't sure how. Can you guide us?"

# *Chapter Thirteen*

Braydon lifted three small pots of roses from his van trunk. Maybe early December wasn't the best time to plant them, but he would give advice, and possibly personal assistance. What the heck, this was for Noelle's mom. Least he could do.

Kerstin rushed out from the community clubhouse where the gardening club met. She wrapped her arms around him, then stepped back in embarrassment.

"Sorry," she said. "I am so excited you are here."

He grinned and put a pot in her arms. "Can you carry that?"

Together they deposited the three pots of

79

gorgeous flowers on the table in front of the small audience of twenty women.

"Good morning," he said. Twenty nods, twenty smiles. This was going to be okay.

An hour later, Kerstin hugged him as he was getting into his van. He had found a fun way to give the rose bushes as prizes. Two women, one gray-haired and another quite young, had won them. Kerstin had won the third, much to his surprise.

"Please, will you help me plant it?" she requested.

"Of course. Will Saturday morning work?"

"Perfect." She hesitated. "Do you mind if Noelle is here?"

"No. As long as she is okay with that." He looked carefully at Kerstin's face. Did she know about the respite? "Please check with her; make sure she is fine with my being there to plant. Okay?"

Kerstin nodded. He decided to accept that as an affirmation.

~

Noelle was excited to help Mom with her garden. It would be like an early Christmas present. She wasn't sure where Mom had gotten the small rose bush she mentioned. But, she thought maybe Braydon had something to do with it, since roses are his specialty. Mostly cut roses, though, in his shop. Still, he did help chose the roses for the Sherman Gardens. Maybe he was a closet cultivator. She chuckled to herself –a new moniker for him.

She arrived at seven just as the sun was peeking from behind clouds of pink fluff. It was blessedly cool, so she pulled her lightweight sweater closer around her shoulders. Instead of parking in front, she swung around to the back and pulled in the driveway. Finally, she had her little red car back, and it looked perfect. The insurance check had come yesterday. This was going to be a good day.

She opened her parents' back door that led into the kitchen and hesitated. She heard voices, male and female. She knew her dad was traveling, so the male voice wasn't his. She would have recognized it anyway. Maybe Uncle Mart? Creeping softly into the kitchen, she thought if it was him she'd give him a silly scare. Like the ones he used to give to her when she was a toddler – big hands covering her eyes from behind, then a cheek peck and "boo!" They would both laugh and hug, and he would swing her high above his head.

The voices faded as if the man and woman were walking through the house to the front door. As she got closer, she distinctly heard Mom say, "I wonder where she is. Not like Noelle to be late."

The male voice responded, sounding familiar. "You sure she won't be upset about this? You did run it by her like you promised, didn't you, Kerstin?"

Mom mumbled something that sounded like, "Forgot."

"Oh, no!" Male voice again. "I'm sure she's going to be upset." Pause. "The respite was her idea, and I've been honoring it."

Braydon! It was his voice, his words. Mom betrayed her.

She put her hand to her throat and spun around.

She almost made it to the back door when a firm masculine hand caught her elbow. "Don't touch me! Take your hand off my arm." She felt herself trembling. Tears pooled in her eyes, and she swiped at them with her knuckles. The toe of her shoe caught the metal strip on the door's threshold, and she grabbed air wildly. Just as she was about to fling forward, strong arms wrapped around her.

"Noelle." Braydon's breath tickled her neck from behind. He chuckled a little. "Please don't pass out this time, beautiful lady. There's no sofa in the kitchen to deposit you on."

"Unhand me." She wiggled loose from his grip and turned to face him. In her nastiest sneer she said, "I thought you were different. You and Mom set me up."

"No, Noelle." Mom's voice drifted across the kitchen. "It's all my fault. Braydon told me about your wish for a respite, and I promised to tell you about him being here." She came up to Noelle with tears on her cheeks. "I forgot."

Noelle looked at her mother whose face was staring at the floor where tears dropped. *Poor Mom. She means well, and she'd never do anything deliberate to hurt me. She is getting older, and don't older people sometimes forget? Even promises.*

She wrapped her arms around Mom. "It's okay. I guess." She hugged Kerstin warmly and kissed her nose. "I know you didn't mean any harm."

Kerstin hugged back and nodded enthusiastically. Her head bobbed up, down and side-ways making Noelle and Braydon laugh. "You look like a bobble-head doll, Mom," she said as she laughed some more.

"I feel like one. Sitting on some idiot's dashboard." She wiped at her eyes with a tissue Noelle handed her.

Noelle decided to be a big girl and let the whole incident go. She knew it wasn't Braydon's fault, and she knew in her heart he was a gentle, caring man with no agenda. Well, maybe one to become her sweetheart. He hadn't grabbed her arm hard, was just trying to delay her to explain the situation. And, he prevented her from falling, maybe even from injuring herself. She had over reacted on both counts. Thanks to her unhealthy relationship with Clay. She had let that go, hadn't she?

"Planting. Aren't we planting?" She eyed her mother and Braydon, both of whom nodded and grinned. "Let's get on with it, then."

She learned from the two of them that Kerstin had won one of the beautiful rose shrubs when Braydon gave a presentation to the Harbor View Garden Club. "Did you fix it to make sure Mom won one of them?"

"Wish I had, but you know that's not my style. It was fair and square. Just luck." He winked. "Or, maybe God's hand was in it so we could plant together." His grin lit up his face, and Noelle felt herself blushing as rosy as the buds on the bush.

The three trooped out to the garden in Kerstin's front lawn. It was a small square patch beyond the hedges bordering the walkway. It was the time of year when the bushes started to produce buds, and

Noelle could see how glorious the colors would be soon when they burst open – crimson, yellow, pale orange, even soft pink with white, lacy tips.

Braydon began to dig; first with a spade, then he dropped to his knees and used a pointed trowel. Noelle heard him mumbling something softly. She squatted down to get closer and hear better.

"Trust in the LORD with all your heart and lean not on your own understanding." He dug deeper.

"I pray that the eyes of your heart may be enlightened in order that you may know the hope to which he has called you, the riches of his glorious inheritance in his holy people ..."

She recognized that scripture from Ephesians. What was he doing? He scooped up a hunk of dirt and deposited it next to the hole he'd dug.

"The grass withers and the flowers fall, but the word of our God endures forever." Isaiah?

Not good at remembering or memorizing Bible verses, she thought she knew where some of the passages came from. Some were from the Old Testament, and some from the New.

She knelt down beside him. He seemed to be in a daze, but very happy.

"See how the flowers of the field grow. They do not labor or spin." He looked content, turned to her and smiled. She felt her face flush and started to put her hand on his. The one holding his trowel. He wore no gloves. She had donned a pair her mother had insisted on giving her. She pulled off the left one and touched his hand.

"You always do this? Recite Bible verses when

you plant?" She looked at him quizzically. He grinned back.

"Yep. Most of the time. Makes me feel like I'm doing something special for the Lord and the land. This is one of my favorites: 'Flowers appear on the earth; the season of singing has come, the cooing of doves is heard in our land.' From Song of Songs."

Noelle could hardly believe it, but she heard birds chirping and doves cooing. She reasoned it was morning when most birds chirped and cooed. Still, had they heard the scripture? She had always loved Song of Songs, the marriage book. She had hoped to have passages read at her wedding. But, that never happened, at least not to abusive Clay. She placed her hand on Braydon's. Did he feel the electricity as she did?

Why was this happening? She wasn't ready for another relationship, at least not this soon, just days from when her former wedding would have happened.

Braydon smiled up at her from his position on the ground. He kept digging and scooping. She was mesmerized. How could this man who owned a floral shop and planted roses have any interest in her? He had run into her car, her BMW baby; he had scooped her up twice, once when she had actually fainted, once when she almost had. He had dined her and given her insight and seemed to really love her mother. Why?

~

Braydon stood up and brushed the damp dirt off the knees of his old corduroy pants. He had forgotten to toss a kneeling pad in his trunk, so good thing he wore the brown trousers. Noelle was slightly bent forward, her manicured fingers resting on her hips. "You could have kept on the gloves and helped," he quipped. He hoped he didn't sound snappish. He reached for her hand.

"I know. It's not that I am uninterested, but I was fascinated watching you." She turned her head and grinned up at him. "I learned a lot, and I loved hearing the Bible verses."

He nodded, and a wide smile spread across his face. "I know it sounds silly, but when I'm planting in a garden or arranging a vase of cut flowers, my concentration is focused. That's when verses leap into my brain." He laughed and clasped her hand. "Concentration is all!"

"Is wet dirt part of it?" She looked down at his mud-splattered hand covering her pristine one and laughed hard.

He laughed back and wiped his hands on one of the towels he'd brought. At least he had remembered to put them in his trunk. "Let me wash up, and we can grab some lunch somewhere."

Noelle gave that some thought while he was in the washroom. She was willing to overlook this morning and Mom's forgetfulness, but she wasn't sure about the rest of the day. Braydon came back grinning and humming. "Ready?"

"I ... I'm not sure we should, Braydon. It's only been a week and a half, and our respite was supposed to be a month." She cocked her head to study his face, the visage that had crumbled and paled. Would he agree? Would he understand?

"Oh," was all he said. He jammed his now clean hands in his pockets and kicked a pebble with the toe of one of his boots. Like a naughty little boy. Like one of her students when she asked for an explanation for misbehavior. Even high school seniors, especially boys, shuffled when uncomfortable. Girls, of course, just started running at the mouth giving ten explanations at once.

"Oh," he said again. This time he shuffled. His behavior was really charming, and it wasn't deliberate or calculated. He was either at a loss for words, or disappointed, or both. It was kind of fun to see a six foot two handsome man bumbling. Men are such characters. She was just about to give in when Mom solved the day.

"Braydon?" Mom stepped out on the walkway. "I'm glad you're still here. Can you join us for lunch? I made Noelle's favorite tuna sandwich on that new pretzel bread."

At least that wouldn't be like a date, just an extension of the morning. This time Noelle grabbed his elbow, gave it a little pinch and led him into the kitchen. They turned to each other and winked. Problem solved.

Mom, however, couldn't let it go. "What's this about a respite? Whose idea was that again?" She searched the two younger faces across the table from her and fiddled with her unnecessary knife.

Braydon and Noelle looked at each other. Both said, "You!"

"You mean you came up with the idea together?" Mom frowned. "Why?"

"No, Kerstin. It was purely your daughter's

idea." Noelle kicked him lightly under the table. Since she was sitting next to him, (thank you, Mom) she only caught his ankle. If she had been across from him she might have kicked him squarely in the shin.

Kerstin looked at Noelle. Noelle shrugged. "Can't you guess?"

"Yes. But, this young man is so different from … most others." She finished lamely and bowed her head. "Oops. We never prayed before taking our first bites. Let's do that now."

Again, Mom's forgetfulness saved the day, or at least the moment.

They were cleaning up the lunch dishes and stacking them in the dishwasher. Braydon had insisted Kerstin sit down and sip her latte, the one with the foam on top she made in her fancy machine. Noelle liked that Braydon inserted the dishes in order, not haphazardly in random, like someone else she had known. She also liked, very much, that he was considerate about Mom. It was hard to find fault with him. He was kind, courteous, gracious, put others ahead of himself, and … handsome. Yet, he never preened or referred to himself to make an impression. Ah, that was it. He is comfortable in his skin, and in his faith.

Her cell phone rang that annoying message, "You are getting a call." She would have to change that, if only she could figure out how.

Her hands were deep in soapy water. As she grabbed a towel to dry them, Braydon asked, "Want me to grab that for you?"

"Sure. But I can't imagine who would be

calling me on a Saturday afternoon during break. Oh, maybe one of the Candy Canes." He looked at her quizzically and tilted his head. "Didn't I tell you about them? I will, soon."

Braydon picked up the phone that was lying on the kitchen counter. "Hello?"

"Who the .... is this? Is this Noelle Day's phone?"

Noelle grabbed the instrument from Braydon. She recognized Bruce Walker's booming, confrontational voice. How had he gotten her cell number? Probably from school records, but those were privileged, only to be used in an emergency.

"Who IS this?" She decided to play dumb.

"It's Bruce, Baby. Your devoted boss." He chuckled, a sound that churned Noelle's stomach. "Hey, who was that who answered? I hope your brother. Oops, you are an only child. Mmm. Dad, uncle maybe?"

Noelle almost gagged that he knew so much about her. As the principal, he had privy to personal records. Still, he had abused them.

She looked to Braydon and Mom for help. She mouthed the words explaining who he was and how he was pursuing her. Braydon looked baffled. Mom didn't.

Kerstin grabbed the phone and in a controlled voice, like a lawyer, said, "Bruce. Kerstin Day here, Noelle's mother. Stop harassing her on the phone, in the parking lot, and stop sending her flowers. NOW." Mom bit her lip. "You are old enough to be her father, and you are acting like a fool. If you don't stop annoying her immediately I will contact

our attorney. You know his name. His daughter is
the same age as Noelle, as is your step daughter."
She took a deep breath, held the phone away from
her ear and practically yelled. "Now, git! Get out
and don't come back. You lech."

# *Chapter Fourteen*

Noelle scooped up Misty and held her close. The little dog nuzzled into Noelle's neck. "Ugh! Misty – wet!" Noelle giggled just as a tiny rough tongue licked her neck. "Enough. I love you, but ..."

She danced around Noelle's feet, front legs raised pawing the air and fluttering. Noelle scooped kibbles and a bit of wet food into the metal dog bowl and set it down in front of the prancing dog.

She was weary, no, tired. She wanted to smash her cell phone and get rid of any memory of Bruce's call. But, she rationalized, it wasn't the phone's fault. There must be a way to block calls from certain people. Tomorrow she would go to one of the nearby phone stores.

She finally drifted off to sleep. What was that chirping sound? Scrambling out of bed and catching her big toe on the sheet, she raced to the kitchen. She always left her cell there, plugged in to be ready for tomorrow. Grabbing at the offending sound to silence it, she looked at the caller ID. Not a number she recognized. But, curiosity took over. If it was Bruce, she would hang up and spit on the phone. She almost laughed at that thought – so dramatic!

The voice on the other end was familiar, and desperate sounding.

"Noelle? It's Cindy." Noelle gasped and waited. Why, at three a.m. was her Candy Cane friend Cindy calling her? "You there?"

"Yes. Something wrong?"

"Yes," came the tearful reply. "It's Doreen. She's been in an accident." Cindy sucked in a deep breath. "She has no family. None. At least not here."

"What?" Noelle couldn't comprehend it. Doreen was always the bubbly one who inspired the rest during competition. She couldn't remember a family, or a group of people, cheering her on like the rest of them had. But, as the anchor on the relay team, she had so much spirit and determination. Surely, she'd had family encouraging her.

Noelle finally found her sleep deprived breath. "What happened? Where? How?" She waited for Cindy to fill her in, tell her what to do, how to help.

"Bad accident on PCH. Maybe you didn't hear the sirens. Just a mile south of you."

"No, I had an exhausting day, fell asleep early. Poor Doreen. How bad is it? Tell me what happened exactly. And, what I can do." Noelle realized she was babbling, but she still wasn't one hundred percent awake. She needed coffee, and her Bible. Doreen needed prayer.

~

It wasn't clear to him why she called him.

Still, he picked her up at four a.m. without a word.

She slid into the passenger seat of his Mercedes and cried. He reached across the console and squeezed her hand. In haste, he hadn't opened the car door for her, thought it more important to get to the hospital. To Doreen.

He didn't know the woman, but he had heard of all the Candy Cane legends – swim team records, mostly. Although he had been two years ahead of Noelle and the Candy Canes, he remembered the girls in the red and white striped swim suits and the whole school cheering them on, even as sophomores. They had almost become legends; cute, even sexy, legends. For some reason he couldn't imagine, he had taken a special shine to the anchor of the relay team, Doreen. Was it because she had an exceptional spirit? Seemed more determined? Of course the anchor on any team had to be the most determined. That person made all the difference, winning or losing.

Braydon pulled into the Hoag Hospital parking lot and this time ran around to help Noelle out of her door. Instinctively, he held her close, briefly. He knew she was sleep deprived, but she smelled so good. Being tuned into the scents of flowers, he thought she smelled like lavender. Not a rose smell, but the scent of some of the trimmings he added to bouquets.

Cindy was curled up in a chair near the now closed hospital gift shop. Her knees were pulled up to her chin and her arms clasped around her shins. Wads of tissues were crumpled in her clamped hands. She jerked her head up when she heard Noelle call her name. Braydon noticed streaks of mascara on Cindy's cheeks. Must be bad for Cindy, the strong one, to be so upset. That's what Noelle had called her, the strong one.

Apparently, she had been the team captain, the one who set the tone and style of the legendary races. Noelle had shared that much on their way to the hospital. It helped him understand more about the chemistry between the girls. Six girls, now women, who still had a special bond after five, or was it six, years? He tried to think about his old surfing friends, his high school buddies and the times they went to Huntington and Trails and even the tip of Balboa. He was still in minimal contact with a few, mainly Gaby, but few others. Maybe guys didn't bond as much. He missed that. At least he had Rob, his brother, even though their interests were vastly different. They kept in touch like the friends they had become.

She jumped up and wrapped her arms around Noelle, held her close and sobbed. Braydon stepped back to investigate the children's artwork hung on the lobby walls. He caught snatches of words between sobs. "Tibia. Might lose leg." That made his forehead wrinkle. Maybe he should learn more, so he could help more. He walked back to the two girls to offer to … what? Do anything that would help.

Noelle's swollen eyes looked forlornly at him. She pulled at his elbow and introduced him to Cindy. Cindy studied his face, then nodded her head. "I remember you. Class clown and debate team. Right?"

Why did everyone remember the class clown part? It was really only that one incident. The one with Coach Wilson. Cindy touched his shoulder and started to laugh.

"Mooning Wilson! That was your defining moment." She swiped at the tears running from her eyes. "I needed that laugh. Thanks, Braydon."

He felt his face color. "I'm glad that memory broke the tension, Cindy." He managed to smile. "Now, tell us what happened and how Noelle and I can help. And, where are the other girls?"

"They will be here eventually, just live further away. I called Noelle first," she explained, "because she lives closest to the hospital."

"Makes sense." He nodded. "I couldn't help overhear the word 'tibia.' Isn't that the bone in the lower part of the leg?"

"Yes. Doreen's is shattered. Might not be reparable, even with surgery. A sliver was sticking out through her skin." She shivered. "She has no family. At least not here in California. After graduation, her parents moved back to their hometown in Wisconsin. Sheboygan."

"What exactly happened? And how, why, were you the one contacted?" Noelle asked in a shaky voice.

"I guess when Doreen filled out an emergency

contact card for her wallet, she listed all of us. Since my last name begins with A, I was called first. You would have been next since you are a D."

"Oh. Go on."

"Well, you know Doreen was always a bit of a dare devil. Not that what she was doing was dare devilish, but if she hadn't been riding her Yamaha scooter, and at night, well ..." Her voice trailed off. Composing herself she continued. "She apparently was making a legal right turn onto Superior when a pickup ran the red light. Knocked her off her scooter and across the street. Head hit the sidewalk curb. Thank goodness she was wearing her helmet."

"And, thank heavens the hospital was so close," Braydon added. "Do you know when they will do surgery? Have you met any of the doctors?"

Cindy shook her head. "No, just nurses and the paramedics who brought her in. She was in horrible pain, as you can imagine. But, was lucid enough to sign a permission form for me to make decisions until her parents arrive." She shook her head again, and tears threatened to spill from her eyes some more. "Poor people. There's not even a major airport near them."

"You talked with them?" Braydon asked.

"Yes. I even managed to hold it together explaining to her dad what happened." She closed her eyes and sighed. "At least with the time difference, it was a decent hour of the morning there." She glanced at Noelle who grinned slightly.

Cindy collapsed again in tears. "I mopped up her blood, the blood dripping constantly from her wound. I had to ask the nurses for extra towels. It was awful."

Braydon couldn't imagine. When he looked at Noelle she was about to collapse. He gripped her arm tight and steered her to a chair. This was horrible news. "You okay? Not good news, but we need to focus on the positive." Was he making any sense, giving the women any hope?

Braydon splashed water on his face in the hospital's lobby restroom. What he thought would be a simple stand by me situation had become a lifeline for Doreen. He knew what he needed to do.

He would have done it for anyone in need, but for Doreen, his lovely Noelle's special friend, it was vital. Not used to demonstrating his faith beyond loved ones, he took a step of faith.

*Please, God, use me.* He felt like Moses, maybe even Aaron. He had never before been so bold asking the Creator to designate him to an assignment. It was scary. It was heavy. It meant he had opened himself to God, completely.

He returned to the hospital lobby and stood before the two girls. Actually women. He had to get that straight in his head. Girls became women, Braydon. Duh. He needed that bit of levity to encourage him.

"Well, Ladies." He hesitated until he got the attention of both. "I have made a decision."

Both looked at him like he was an alien. He laughed and took a hand of each in his.

~

The surgery for Doreen had taken more than the predicted five hours. It actually lasted almost seven grueling hours.

Noelle, Cindy and Braydon knelt in the hospital's small chapel. They had clasped sweaty hands for hours.

A nurse came in and said, "It is over. You can go see her in recovery." Then she left.

Stiffly they all sat up. It was almost surreal. They looked at each other in confusion. What would they find, what would they learn? Why hadn't the nurse told them more?

"She came through the surgery very well," the doctor wearing the surgical mask now under his chin said. "By the way, I am Doctor Melborn. Sorry, I hadn't met with you before. Long, busy night," he gave as an explanation.

"What do you mean *very well*?" Braydon asked.

"I think I can predict she will keep her leg. It was a touch and go situation."

Braydon frowned. "What does 'that' mean?"

"It means if she is strong and heals well, she will be fine. But," he added, "after a lot of physical therapy. Months." He tilted his head, then added. "We had to put a rod in her leg to stabilize it. That leg will be slightly shorter than the other. A few pins, too."

"Doc. Do you know she is a swimmer, an almost Olympic swimmer? Her legs mean everything to her future. She is also a swim coach."

Doc Melborn shook his head. He didn't know. "No one told me. Sorry."

None of them could fault the guy. He had done the best he knew how to do. A wonderful surgeon. God had blessed them with him, and Braydon told him so.

Doreen's parents arrived.

They had taken a cab from John Wayne Orange County Airport straight to Hoag Hospital. Braydon and the girls surrounded the weary couple with hugs and love. The other Candy Canes had arrived a few hours ago, right after Noelle, Cindy and Braydon had visited a groggy Doreen in recovery. Fortunately, she still wasn't totally cognizant which helped them avoid her hard questions. Cindy was relieved to pass the baton, so to speak, to Doreen's parents about health decisions. Although she consulted with Noelle and Braydon, whom she trusted now, she felt a bit inadequate in the role Doreen had assigned her.

All the girls heard that Doreen would need intense physical therapy for a long time. They had mulled it over and discussed how they could help. Maybe driving her to it, providing meals, even having her stay temporarily with one of them.

Natalie spoke up first during their discussion. "When the physical therapists pronounce her able, she can work out at my gym – free ... forever." The other four girls stared at her.

"And, because my schedule is flexible, I will drive her," Connie said. The girls all grinned and high-fived each other. They still honored their bond.

When Doreen's parents heard about the arrangements her mother started to weep, and her dad wiped at his eyes with his knuckle. "You girls are so sweet," Mrs. Zimmer said. "We plan on taking her back home with us."

"NO!" They all shouted at once. "She belongs here," Connie said a bit too loudly. "I already have an idea for her, for employment." The parents and the Candy Canes all gazed at Connie with questioning eyes.

"I work for a huge design firm, even design some of its specialty lines." She stopped to focus on the faces before her. "We have been seeking a new angle for a new line. She can be our model."

Six pairs of eyes looked at her questioningly. Doreen model with a gimp leg? How was that possible. Her mother asked that question.

"The fashion line I'm planning is for women with disabilities." She looked around at all those faces, but continued. "No, Doreen's is not, will not be, a huge disability. Not like a woman with an amputated leg. But, it's a start." She chuckled. "Always start small."

Mrs. Zimmer clasped her hands and grinned. "What a great solution!" She hugged Connie, then held her at arm length. "Would that make her feel inadequate, less?"

"Not at all, Mrs. Zimmer. It will make her a star for every young girl or woman who is dealing with a physical disability. She will look elegant in every gown, in every outfit. She will be a great poster girl."

"Now," Cindy said, "we just have to convince Doreen."

"Let's go to the chapel and pray about it." Noelle said. She led the way.

# *Chapter Fifteen*

"I don't know what to do," the charge nurse approached the little group with her hands wringing.

Braydon was the first to reach for her shaking hands and clasped them. "What is wrong? Is Doreen all right?"

She nodded. "Her vital signs seem okay, but she is semi-awake now, and she keeps asking for Candy Canes. But, I know she is not allowed to have any candy or sweets."

Eight people burst into laughter. The poor nurse was more confused than ever. "Why are you all laughing?"

"I think, I believe," Braydon said, "she is asking for her friends. The Candy Canes."

He bit his lip when he realized the nurse didn't understand. Then, he started to explain.

Noelle stepped forward. "She is asking for her friends, her special friends. We are a group called the Candy Canes."

"Oh." The nurse still seemed confused. Cindy stepped forward next and attempted to explain the old swim team and its camaraderie.

"Swimming … candy canes?" Nurse shook her head. "Did you eat them before a swim meet? Or celebrate with them after?"

Even Doreen's mother giggled at that image. "No, dear," she said to the nurse and touched her arm. "Their swim suits had red and white stripes like candy canes. Their coach named them the Candy Canes. And, the whole school picked up on the moniker."

The nurse nodded and grinned, blushing a little. Poor thing is embarrassed Noelle thought. Not her fault.

"I understand now." She said. "Oh, she is asking for all of you. But, we aren't supposed to allow more than two visitors at a time." She looked perplexed again.

"We can go in two by two," Cindy said. "We sometimes swam that way. In practice," she added.

Cindy and Noelle went in first. The others followed. After everyone, including Braydon and Doreen's mother went in as team, things settled down. It was then they realized Doreen's father had been left out of the loop since he had been getting coffee in the hospital cafeteria during all the decisions about visiting Doreen.

Noelle felt terrible. If it had been her dad in her compromised health situation, she would have been devastated. She grabbed Mr. Zimmer's hand and pulled him forward.

After explaining to the charge nurse, the woman made an exception, "But, just for a few minutes."

The tall, gray haired man stepped forward and released Noelle's hand. "I want to do this alone," he said. Noelle nodded.

~

It was getting late, and everyone was exhausted. Doreen's parents showed signs of wilting after their long trip and their concern for her. Braydon offered to drive them to the hotel they had made reservations at. Fortunately, it was just a few miles from Hoag Hospital and on the way to Noelle's.

Noelle climbed in back with Doreen's mother, and her dad sat up front with Braydon. Mrs. Zimmer gave Noelle's hand a squeeze. "I like your young man," she said. "He's not the one ...?" She stumbled over her question, but Noelle knew what she was asking.

"No, not *that* one." She smiled at the older woman to reassure her.

"I ... I didn't know how to ask. Sorry."

"It's really okay, Mrs. Zimmer. A blessing," she said. "One of those 'in disguise' ones." She actually found herself giggling a bit and laid her hand on the woman's arm.

"So glad. I was afraid I'd offend you." She hesitated. "I understand from Doreen you did a brave thing cancelling the wedding."

"Yes, it was difficult." She leaned close to Mrs.

Zimmer and whispered, filling her in about how she'd met Braydon, how he'd been the chosen florist for her cancelled nuptials. "We just started to see each other, no official dates. But, he does seem to be a special man. Christian, too," she added with a grin.

They pulled into the long drive of the Hyatt, and Noelle's hands started to sweat. It was the hotel where she and Clay were supposed to get married.

Braydon sensed her discomfort. After all, he had spent hours at the hotel with its onsite wedding coordinator making floral decisions for the wedding. He turned his head to glance at the back seat and winked and received a weak smile from the girl he was sure he was falling in love with.

# *Chapter Sixteen*

Noelle kicked off her boots, flinging them under the coat rack. She wiggled her toes in relief, then pulled off the socks sending them to land on the tips of the leather toes. Collapsing on the sofa, she placed her bare heels on the edge of the coffee table just as her cell phone rang. Who on earth? Not Braydon. He had just left, and his name didn't come up. Maybe Doreen's parents? But, it was a local number. She decided not to answer. If the caller wanted to leave a message, she would pick it up later. Much later.

It had been so nice to connect with Doreen's mother, even in tragedy. She remembered they had met before, a few times during swim competitions and before her parents had moved back to their hometown in Montana. But, they had never been close, never bonded like so many of the girls had done with her parents. Maybe because her family was local and Mom had often invited the girls for meals. Mom had this thing about wanting to make sure all the girls ate well, especially since after graduation so many of their parents had moved away to retire in Arizona, Colorado and some in Florida.

She closed her eyes and drifted back in time. She saw the lineup, the six girls in striped suits wiggling and rubbing their hands together and slapping their knees and pulling at their swim caps. Those were exciting moments. Teen moments. But, because of the bond they held, because of Coach Douglas's faith in them, those moments had become forever moments.

Just as she was drifting off to a much needed nap, her land line rang. This time she couldn't ignore it when the tinny voice said "Carson, Melanie." Bruce's stepdaughter. Noelle remembered her from high school, actually before her mother married the principal. Melanie had always seemed a bit sad, not very social. Of course, since she didn't swim, they only saw each other in a few classes. Why was she calling? Hopefully, Bruce hadn't put her up to it.

"What do you want?" Noelle held the phone away from her ear and glared at it. Why was Melanie calling her? She had barely spoken to the girl before. Weird.

The words on the other end stumbled. The woman was obviously upset. Was Bruce behind this? What part was he playing in his stepdaughter calling her?

"Please don't hang up, Noelle, please," the shaky voice on the other end pleaded. "I ... I called to find out how your friend is." Noelle could hear the woman was crying. "I was the one that hit her," she sobbed. "It was me."

"Oh. How did you get my number?" She could only imagine. And why was that more important than why Melanie had called? Priorities, Noelle, priorities.

"You sound very upset." Brilliant, Noelle. "What can I do for you?"

"May I come see you? To talk with you in person?"

Noelle bit her lip and hesitated before she responded. This woman was obviously in pain. Of course not the kind of pain Doreen was experiencing. After a long pause and another plaintive "please" from the woman on the other end of the call, she simply said, "Why?"

She felt like a heel. Was she reluctant because Melanie was Bruce Walker's stepdaughter? Or, would she have hesitated no matter who she was?

"Because ..." Noelle heard a choking sound on the other end. "Because I need to talk with someone, need someone to pray with me." Pause. "I heard you are a Christian." Another pause. "Bruce told me."

Noelle swallowed hard. If only Melanie weren't connected to Bruce. If only. Still, it wasn't Melanie's fault her mother had married the disgusting man. She sounded sincere, and very troubled. Finally, she sighed and consented. Why not? Was the Lord leading her? She hoped so. Isn't that what her devotions yesterday morning had centered on? Being a friend, two praying together? Helping one another.

"Yes, Melanie. Come."

"Thank you so much," was almost buried in another flood of tears and choking.

Noelle opened her door reluctantly. What, or who, would she find there? She had made a fresh pot of coffee and had the kettle on for tea. She also had soft drinks in the fridge. And Shortbread cookies from the bakery, even the Gelson's bakery. Such an indulgence. She wanted to get the girl, why did she keep referring to her as a girl, to open up and be comfortable.

As it turned out, Melanie was a sobbing mess.

"Thank you for seeing me," she said as she collapsed into Noelle's arms. She was shaking so hard Noelle didn't know what to do to calm her. Finally, she hugged her – hard. And led her to the sofa pushing extra cushions around her. Sweet Misty saved the day when she jumped on Melanie's lap.

Noelle started to berate the dog, but Melanie whispered, "No. Please. She is so adorable, and she seems to like me," she said as Misty licked at her tears.

"So." She looked at Melanie. "You like dogs? You have one?"

"No," the other woman said sadly. "Bruce is allergic. But," she continued, "I've always wanted one."

"They are great companions. Always there when we need them. Very loyal."

Melanie nodded and reached for a tissue from the box Noelle had strategically placed on the coffee table.

Noelle offered drinks, and Melanie accepted coffee while she was reaching for a cookie. Progress. Noelle felt a quilt twinge. She had nothing personally against the other woman, except she had confessed she was the one who ran into Doreen.

"So," she said guardedly, "you caused the accident?"

More sobbing. Finally, Melanie got control and set down her coffee cup. "Yes. It was me."

"Wanna tell me about it? You did come here to share, right?"

# *Chapter Seventeen*

**W**hat a horrible evening!

Melanie's story was very sad. Almost as sad as her causing Doreen's accident. Noelle opened her Bible to James. She knew there were passages about asking for direction in life, and she needed them now.

*Everyone should be quick to listen, slow to speak and slow to become angry, ...*

She rolled that verse over in her mind. She thought she had followed it. She had patiently listened to Melanie's confession, kept her ordinarily blabbering mouth shut, and found it was hard to be angry at the other woman. The woman who had changed her friend's life.

Closing The Book, she called Braydon. She wasn't sure why. Why not Mom who was always her Biblical advisor? She didn't question, just pushed the right buttons on her cell.

Braydon answered on the quick. Was he expecting her? Now, her blabbering overflowed. And, he listened without interruption.

~

Braydon had mixed feelings. Was he convenient? Yet, he felt blessed that Noelle called him and shared. He, too, was confused about the Melanie confession. Did she just have the need to confess to someone? From everything Noelle had shared, he believed Melanie was truly repentant. Apparently, from what she's said to Noelle, she had no church home, maybe hadn't gone to one for years. Bruce's influence?

He wanted to pray with Noelle over the phone, but being there in person was so much better.

Better yet would be to pray with Melanie. Finally, he decided and called Noelle back. Would she understand?

"Oh, I guess. Okay. I will call her to come back. You sure?" she asked.

~

Braydon settled on Noelle's sofa and waited. He held a cup of coffee between his hands to warm them. Finally, the doorbell rang.

Noelle led another woman by the hand and sat her next to Braydon on the couch. She seemed very uncomfortable, hugging her arms against herself tightly.

Braydon didn't even acknowledge her, just took her hand in his. He knew. He had trusted his savior to lead this woman to him, and now to Him.

Although he didn't know all the details, he knew from Noelle this was the person who had caused Doreen's devastating accident, the one that would change her life forever.

He knew none of the facts, but that was okay. He just started to pray.

He closed his eyes. "Dear Heavenly Father." He felt a shiver, and the hand he was holding almost pulled away. But, he held on. "We know You are supreme. You know every outcome of every situation. We trust You completely to find the peace and comfort we need." He paused and bowed his head. "Please bless our friend Melanie who is sad, confused and needing Your comfort." He bowed his head lower. "Please draw her close to You, Lord. Let her feel your presence in a powerful way."

Braydon felt the hand clasped in his released. Had he confused her? Said the wrong prayer? No, he trusted God for the words. He knew the understanding would come later. Sometimes it took time. God's time.

Was this God's time for him and Noelle? He set his coffee cup down and pulled her close. This evening had been very dramatic and enlightening, and he felt closer to Noelle than ever. He wanted her so badly. Is that why God was encouraging him? He knew he had fallen in love with her, but how did she feel? He decided to risk and pressed his lips to hers. They were sweet and tasted of coffee and cookies. Again, she smelled like lavender. He clung to the softness of her lips, and when finally forcing himself to break away, he hugged her again and grinned. He composed himself and strode to the door. When he heard it click, he knew. This was the real thing!

The next day the Candy Canes and Braydon and Melanie trooped into the hospital. The poor charge nurse was speechless. Braydon thought she might faint. He approached her very delicately with outstretched hands.

"I remember all of you," she said with a shaky voice. "Candy Canes?"

Braydon laughed and nodded. Just for fun, and because it was the Christmas season, he handed her a fistful of striped candy canes. She collapsed in laughter.

This time she ignored how many of them went to Doreen's room. Doreen was propped up in bed, TV on, but eyes closed. Cindy pushed the off button on the remote, and Doreen's eyes flew open. "Oh, my!" She scanned the group, and gave them a weak smile. "All of you." Then she noticed Melanie. "Who are you? Do I know you?"

Melanie shook her head, and strands of brown tresses clung to tears on her cheeks. She approached Doreen gingerly, very slowly, glancing toward the group behind her. All the girls and Braydon nodded. She reached for the tissue box next to the hospital bed and pulled one out. Dabbing at her face, she pulled her shoulders back, raised her chin and laid her hand on Doreen's arm. Connie let out a little gasp and grabbed Candy's arm. Noelle reached for Braydon's hand and bowed her head.

Finally, Melanie spoke. "It was me."

Doreen frowned. "You? What? I don't

understand."

"Me. The one who ran into you."

"Oh." Doreen pulled her arm away and turned her head. "Why?"

"Why did I come here? I'm not sure. Felt the need," she whispered, "to confess."

Braydon and Noelle touched the others' arms and gestured for all of them to leave Melanie and Doreen alone. They slipped out quietly, closing the door behind them.

"What now?," Natalie asked.

"Now," Braydon said, "we pray."

# *Chapter Eighteen*

The Night Before the Night Before Christmas

Kerstin checked the antique sideboard in her large dining room. She counted the stack of Spode soup bowls for the third time, and ran her hand along the edge of the embroidered linen runner they sat on. She could hardly wait for all the guests to arrive. The Honey Baked Ham Soup she and Noelle had made was keeping warm in her biggest Crockpot. Noelle and Candy had made the tiny corn muffins yesterday, and they were nestled in a linen Christmas napkin in a woven silver basket. This is why she had collected the Christmas china for so many years; this is why she clung to the big house on the hill – to entertain, especially at holidays, and especially young people. She wasn't ready to downsize yet as Darrell had hinted at for several years. No, she loved her Newport enclave. Her Bible study and garden club friends were here, and amazingly, so were all of Noelle's Candy Cane friends. Now, Braydon. How she hoped, and prayed.

Noelle, Natalie and Candy checked the sign they had printed out and hung on the giant basket by the front door. They tossed their wrapped items in it and giggled just as the doorbell chimed. Noelle always got a kick out of that chime. Somehow her mother and dad had figured out how to change its tune for special occasions. This evening it played Jingle Bells, God Rest Ye Merry Gentlemen and Joy to the World alternately. Since these were the first guests to arrive Jingle Bells permeated the air.

It was a cool California evening. No snow, of course. But, thankfully, cool enough for light jackets. Cindy and Connie shrugged off their shawls and following Noelle's lead dropped their tiny wrapped packages in the big basket. Soon, the other Candy Canes came in laughing and bumping against each other.

Last came Doreen with her parents. She was on crutches wrapped in red and green tape. She had only been released from the hospital this morning. But, her smile was huge, and her parents beamed. Mrs. Zimmer handed Noelle a plastic medicine container. "Can you please set a timer? Doreen needs to take a pill at seven."

The guest list was complete. Almost.

Where was Dad?

And Braydon? She touched her lips where he had kissed her so passionately the other evening after Melanie had left. His lips had clung to hers, and she'd found her own clinging back. She remembered the heady taste of coffee and the Shortbread cookie he'd devoured mixed with the subtle smell of flowers. "My candy cane rose," he had called her. Maybe she was now officially a GF.

Noelle started to fume until her mother put a hand on her arm. "Dad had to run an errand, and maybe Braydon had a last minute floral order." Kerstin offered. "They will probably be along soon."

The bell chimed Joy to the World, and Noelle rushed to the door to open it. Then, she stopped, and stared. Melanie?

"I hope I'm not too late. It was so kind of your mother to invite me." She held a small wrapped package in one hand. "Where should I put this?" Noelle gestured to the big basket.

Noelle forced a smile. "Of course not. Please come in," she said as politely as possible while gritting her teeth. Mom had invited Melanie? The woman who had caused Doreen's devastating accident? What was she thinking?

Just as she was about to be surly, Doreen's mother and Kerstin rushed to the door and each took one of Melanie's hands. Mrs. Zimmer hugged her, and Kerstin planted a kiss on her cheek.

What is happening here? Most people who cause accidents don't usually attend celebrations that include the person they hurt. Why did Mom invite her? Why was Doreen's mother so kind?

Doorbell.

This time Cindy answered. And shrieked.

A portly Santa Clause with an askew beard boomed "Ho, ho, ho!"

Everyone burst into laughter as he adjusted his whiskers. They all clapped as he waddled into the foyer. He held a black trash bag tied at the top and started to fiddle with it.

"Let me help you, Santa," Kerstin said as she stepped forward. She undid the yellow plastic ties and spread open the bag. Santa winked at her.

He reached into his bag and pulled out a fuzzy teddy bear. Then he made an announcement.

"Ho, ho, ho." His eyes twinkled. Noelle knew Dad was having fun. "Each of you will get a bear; each has the name of an organization on a tag around its neck." He paused to survey the group to make sure he had everyone's attention. When he was sure, he went on. "It will be your responsibility tomorrow to help Santa deliver your teddy bear to the organization on your bear's tag. So," he continued, "a child they sponsor will get a bear." He looked around to smiling faces. "Okay with that?"

Everyone clapped and some hooted. What a delightful Santa. He passed out bears, tore off his beard to reveal Noelle's dad and started peeling off the heavy red suit just as …

The doorbell rang again.

Kerstin rushed to the door this time. She had a feeling who might be there as she swung it open.

Yep, another Santa. But, more authentic. He pushed his way in, like he belonged. His attire was perfect, could have played the part in a Hollywood film. Beard clung to his chin naturally, even eyebrows were white and fluffy. Black gloves, black boots – not fake. He raised those perfect white brows and looked around slowly, taking his time.

Finally, he spoke. There was a corporate sigh of relief from all the guests. Maybe some thought he was an intruder. But, Kerstin knew better.

"Ho, ho, ho." He paused again and looked at the guests. "I think I'm supposed to say that." Giggles. "I am not here to pass out gifts to all." A group sigh. "Sorry to disappoint you, but I think you will understand, and be pleased." He looked around again, then stopped.

"I am searching for a future Mrs. Santa. Anyone available? It comes with a lot of work. Supervising elves, checking lists, washing and ironing my red uniform." He stopped there. "Well, I can do that myself. My mother, the Grandma Santa taught me how." He grinned. "I guess the only other thing is to love me.

"Any takers?" He looked directly at Noelle.

"Did I mention I love little dogs? Especially ones with long tails."

Kerstin clasped her hands together. This was so special, more than what she had prayed for. Darrell put his arm around her. The Candy Canes reached out to each other and embraced hands. One of them, Doreen maybe, reached for Melanie's hand. Doreen's parents had no clue what was happening, but they held hands and smiled. Anticipation?

Santa stumbled toward Noelle who was sitting on the sofa, her forehead in her hands nodding back and forth. He landed onto one knee and held up a blue velvet jewelry box.

"Will you, Noelle, be my Mrs. Santa? To have and to hold forever, and to check lists and supervise elves? Maybe help deliver flowers and make sure gift cards are in perfect English?"

Noelle collapsed in such hearty laughter everyone was stunned into silence. Even Santa Braydon. "Did I say it wrong?"

"No, no," she said choking back laughter and tears. "It was perfect." Still laughing, she reached for his hand.

The soup was succulent, brimming with chunks of ham and loaded with beans. Noelle added more onions. The cornbread muffins melted in mouths. The most fun part was the ornament exchange, the little wrapped items tossed in the big basket by the door. It was a tradition in Noelle's family. Bring an ornament with tag attached to explain what it meant to the giver; take an ornament and enjoy.

Noelle lifted the one she had chosen to a high branch on her parents' tree. A tiny red pickup truck. Written on the door were the words in permanent marker "Forgiven."

# *Epilogue*

## One Year Later

Melanie fussed with her skirt. She laid her heart-shaped bouquet on the sofa in the Garden's ante room, grabbed a tissue and dabbed at her lashes. Doreen took her hand. "It's okay, Melanie. All is forgiven. Please don't cry and ruin your makeup."

Melanie nodded and smiled. She was so grateful for Doreen's forgiveness and for God's.

"Oh, here they all come!" she squealed with delight. Four perfumed women raced up the steps of the Sherman Foundation Gardens and burst with giggles into the room reserved for the bridal party. Red taffeta crinkled its own special tune. Cindy twirled and Natalie spun like a human top, one held arms outstretched holding her bouquet, the other with manicured hands pointing to the ceiling.

"Oh, we almost didn't make it on time. Parking lot is super full. Then Cindy noticed the reserved signs in the first row," Connie said breathlessly. "Thank goodness Braydon lent us his van so we could all come together." In the next gulp she said, "We hope those spaces were reserved for the wedding party."

"Then," Candy took up the slack, "we had to decorate the groom's car. Without scratching it," she finished in a gasp. "Can't scratch a Mercedes." The girls all giggled.

"I hope you didn't do anything really bad." Doreen frowned at them. "Like put a raw fish on the engine."

"No, no, never. Not 'that' bad." Cindy assured them. "I heard about how the male attendants at Noelle's Uncle Mart's wedding did that. Awful! By the time he and her Aunt Susan got to the airport, in of all cars her dad's Caddy, the engine was almost ruined." She screwed up her face. "And it stunk!" All the girls whooped with laughter.

Melanie felt so blessed to be included in this special group of friends, and especially in the wedding. It had taken a bit of research on Noelle's part to find an exact replication of the dresses that were purchased over a year ago for the 'first' wedding. If anyone chose to measure, her white sash was almost an inch narrower than the others. She didn't care. These women were amazing how they had taken her under their collective wings, and especially how Doreen had forgiven her. Doreen with the now shorter leg.

She was so glad she had moved away from her

mother and Bruce. Thankful, too, that he was in therapy for his overly fondness for young women. Her mother who believed in her vows, even after her widowhood from Melanie's father, was hanging in there with him. She was grateful he had taken an administrative job, leaving his principal position at VDM. The new female principal was kind and nurturing and right up front.

"Say ..." She shook herself out of her reverie and looked around at the radiant faces. "Anyone know where the bride is?"

Just then the door opened and Kerstin and Darrell walked in with the groom's parents. She had never met them before, but some of the Candy Canes had. A tall man with silver gray hair escorted a naturally blond woman, petite and delicate looking. "Hi, girls. My, you are all so beautiful," he said with a warm smile.

"I do love the red," Mrs. Lovejoy smiled, too. "It reminds me of the special Splash of Red rose at The Garden."

"Do you think, Mrs. Lovejoy, that we look like candy canes?" Natalie couldn't resist asking.

"Yes. Actually, you look like Candy Cane roses." She tipped her head. "Do you like your bouquets?"

A collective sigh. Echoes of "Beautiful!" and "Gorgeous!" and "Heavenly!" ricocheted around the room. Mrs. Lovejoy looked very pleased. "I designed them," she offered. "I wanted them to be exceptional for this wedding, the wedding I've been praying for," she squeeze a tissue in her hand, "for almost thirty years."

She scanned the group of girls, and her gaze rested on Doreen. "You," she pointed a delicate finger, "must be the Maid of Honor." She tilted her head again. "So tall and elegant." She focused on Doreen again. "I figured it out because your gown is slightly different. Longer." Mrs. Lovejoy seemed pleased with herself to have made that distinction.

Melanie grabbed Doreen's hand and squeezed. Doreen shook her head, and the chignon clasped on its crown wiggled a little. "It's okay, Mel," she whispered. She stepped forward to touch the other woman's hands. "I *am* different, but only by about an inch and a half," she chuckled.

Melanie noticed the confused expression on Mrs. Lovejoy's face. She prayed she would take Doreen's explanation graciously and not be embarrassed. She had forgotten how tactful Doreen was, how humble. It would be all right.

There was so much silence in the room. Every girls' eyes were focused on Doreen and Mrs. Lovejoy. Doreen explained to Braydon's mother in a stage whisper; then, they hugged. Everyone clapped. It was going to be okay.

Kerstin stepped forward dapping at her own eyes. "It's almost time, girls."

"But," several said in unison, "where is the bride?"

"I am here!" Noelle swished into the room in possibly the most elegant gown any of them had ever seen, even in magazines. She, too, twirled with hands above her head and holding a huge trailing bouquet of striped roses with silver glitter on the pedals. Gorgeous! And, the gown was strapless! No bruises, no yellow marks. Cindy and Melanie clasped their hands and bowed their heads. God is so good, they both whispered.

All the girls fussed over her, careful not to touch her gorgeous gown. But, finally, Natalie asked where she found it.

"Super simple. Connie designed it. Isn't it beautiful?"

## Noelle

I am overwhelmed. I can't even fathom this day, Lord. I know, I am using advanced English teacher lingo. Should have used the word 'understand.' Still, one of my future duties is to decipher letters to Santa, no matter how the words are used or spelled or misspelled. I know that is just a fantasy, but a fun one.

I hear the music drifting in, the harp playing, and my precious friend Sandy is singing in Braydon's and my honor. I asked her to sing Joy to the World, to remind everyone about the joy of the Savior, and the joy of my marriage. She is singing it perfectly, with joy.

Braydon and I chose a long walk for me to reach him, past the central garden where most of the guests are seated, and it will end at the small rose portion of the garden. We will say our vows privately there, then he will take my hand and escort me back past our guests to the Central Patio Room. There we will celebrate. Yippee!

I clasp my gorgeous and enormous trailing bouquet to my face. Its scent overwhelms me. The roses are striped, like candy canes. Each petal is tipped in silver glitter. I know Braydon designed this just for me. How will I ever make it up to him?

Oh, I know. Being Mrs. Santa. I can do that!

Actually, I found out from pressing him that Love In Bloom has a Santa Letter division it promotes at Christmas time. Local kids, any kids anywhere, can write a letter to Santa, and we will answer it. That is one of my new jobs! Such fun.

Dad takes my hand. I take his arm. The Lohengrin wedding march begins. Suddenly, I tremble. I look into Dad's eyes. He nods. "This is right, Noelle. So right," he says, a smile embracing his face, mistiness clouding his eyes. Together we step forward.

~

Braydon shifted on his feet, the ones in rented wedding shoes. It wasn't that he wasn't sure, but, was she? She had finally confessed to him about Clay's, her former fiancé's, abuse. It was still confusing to him why she would even allow that. But, after talking with her mother Kerstin, he had a better understanding. Now, he trusted. Her, and the Lord.

Jill, the former, now current wedding coordinator again, touched his arm and nodded. It was time. He moved from the little room reserved for the male attendants and walked to the small rose garden area. He would wait there for his bride.

## The End

May your life be filled with candy cane moments.

Enjoy the first chapter of book two,
Cindy's Perfect Dance.

*C*indy dug through the cardboard carton. She pulled out fistfuls of old photographs from over twelve years ago. She dug deeper, hoping to find "the one." Finally, she thought she had it, the black and white one of Rob. How she wished she'd had the money to buy the yearbooks before her own graduation. But, her parents were cash-strapped, and she worked during after school hours as a barista at Starbucks. So, some of those years were lost, at least in photos. It was before everyone had cell phones they could store photos in.

She held the blurry photo up to the light. Was Rob really that handsome then? He looked goofy in the image. But, so did the other guys hugging each other's' shoulders. Must have been taken after a track meet. In those days the date of the photograph was noted on the back. Four years before she had graduated.

She found another photo. *Oh, my gosh, almost forgot he was voted class king. He deserved it, but he is so humble now.* She rubbed her eyes and sat down. She could hardly believe she was dating a former class king of Vista del Mar High School. He had never mentioned it. But, that was so teenage, so juvenile. He was all grown up now. Really grown up.

She'd had a huge crush on Rob when she was only starting into her freshman year. He had never seemed to flaunt his kingship, or any of his academic accolades or sports accomplishments. But, she followed them. She knew.

She threw the photos aside, tossing them haphazardly on her kitchen table. What had happened the other evening at Noelle and Braydon's wedding? Her Candy Cane best friend had married a florist. The owner of the floral shop that was previously contracted to provide the flowers for Noelle's original wedding, the one she cancelled because of her former fiancé Clay's abuse. Last night, almost a year later, was a beautiful event. It was after the ceremony when the couple had been toasted and the small ensemble started to play dance music. That's when Rob gently grasped her hand and led her to the area by the pond at the entrance of the Sherman Gardens. That's when she melted in his arms.

He held her close and started to dance, very slowly. His nose nestled in her ear. The little band was playing that old tune "Someday My Prince Will Come" from Disney's Snow White. The singer was crooning in an old fashioned way. "Cynthia," he whispered hoarsely. Cindy thought her heart would leap out of her bridesmaid's gown as red as the taffeta skirt. She snuggled closer.

Suddenly, the band switched to "Santa, Baby,"

perfect for this Christmas wedding. But, the faster beat seemed to catch Rob off guard. The song was especially perfect since Braydon the groom had proposed to Noelle in a Santa costume at her parents' Christmas party last year. What a hoot that had been. He had been very authentic, even though everyone knew it was him. Noelle had been so overcome with joy she laughed and cried at the same time. What a memory. She had agreed to be Mrs. Santa supervising elves and answering children's letters to the jolly red-clad elf. In perfect English, using her skills as an English teacher.

Cindy shook her head and laughed softly. "What? What did you say, Rob?"

"I said 'Let's go to the parking lot where we can twirl.'" He looked at her quizzically. "You okay being with me?"

"Oh, yes. Forgive me. I was thinking about how your brother proposed to Noelle last Christmas." She pressed closer to him. "I'm sorry, but it was such a treat to see. Too bad you weren't there. You would have loved it."

Rob nodded, somewhat unenthusiastically. "Braydon always was the melodramatic one, the clever one, the one who always managed to get into some kind of trouble or do something dramatic." He sounded jealous, then clasped her hand again. "So, would you? Like to go to the parking lot where we have more room to dance?"

Cindy nodded, then asked, "Should we? Aren't we supposed to stay with the wedding party? And the guests." She could see he wasn't convinced. He was the Best Man, so shouldn't he be available for the rest of the event?

"I suppose. But, maybe just a few minutes where there is more space, and," he added with a wink, "where we will be more alone."

Cindy wasn't so sure, but it was hard to deny this man. Like his brother, Braydon the groom, he was handsome, but different. Instead of blue eyes like Braydon's, his were hazel, the kind that turned subtle colors – pale brown, even green sometimes. Depending on the light. His face wasn't sculptured like Braydon's, but it was definitely handsome. Especially graced by that full head of luxurious brown hair. Why was she comparing him? It was hard not to because the brothers were so different in stature and coloring. She had expected Robinson to look like a twin to Braydon. Yet, he never had in high school. Maybe she was having a memory lapse.

She took his offered hand and held up her red taffeta skirt so she wouldn't trip. When they reached the parking lot lined with cars, she realized he was right. There was a huge area in the middle. They danced.

She wasn't sure what song was playing because the music barely drifted that far. But, he lived up to his promise, and they twirled. And twirled more, until she was almost dizzy. It was almost magical. She had never expected this somewhat humble and sometimes shy man to be such a marvelous dancer. Definitely a hidden talent. Until now.

Breathless, she laid her hand on his arm. "Rob, I have to stop." He looked at her with a question in his eyes. "I have to use the bathroom!"

"Oh."

"Sorry. Meet you back at the reception. K?"

He nodded. She raced up the low steps holding her skirt again. He followed slowly.

~

The reception was winding down. It was almost midnight. A few guests had left, leaving empty spaces at the round tables. Suddenly, the band played a loud drum roll. The leader approached the microphone and laughed. "Ladies and gentlemen, it is time. Time for all the fun stuff. The groom will toss the garter, if he can find it, and the bride will toss her bouquet." He looked around and snickered. "All single men form a circle around Braydon."

About twenty men and boys shuffled forward. Cindy pushed Rob who protested. "But, I'm his brother. I shouldn't be there."

"You're single, right? Or, am I mistaken?" She pushed him again. Reluctantly, he tried to fade into the group.

The band did a staccato drum beat. Braydon made a big show of trying to find Noelle's garter. Cindy knew it was below her knee because Noelle was embarrassed even having one. But, being a good sport, she played along. Braydon fumbled and pretended to search for it. Noelle giggled when he lifted the skirt of her gown and stuck his head under. He groped, she kicked. Was she going to kick him in the face, the face under her skirt? Finally, he held a blue garter above his head with an impish grin. He swung it around on a finger. Twenty plus pairs of male hands waved in the air. His eyes locked on one, and he aimed. Right at his brother.

Rob had no choice but to catch it. It practically flew into his hands. His face burned crimson, but he held it tight against his chest. A few of the men moaned, but many clapped him on the back. "Your time, buddy. Congratulations, guy." Cindy grinned.

More drum beats, another announcement. "Now, ladies, form a circle. The bride is going to toss her beautiful bouquet." The announcer stopped. "Oops, sorry. She wants to preserve her real bouquet. But, the one she is going to toss is special. Reach to catch."

Cindy was glad Noelle wouldn't toss the gorgeous bouquet Braydon had designed just for her. However, she noticed the one in Noelle's raised hand was also outstanding. That Braydon. He would be sure every floral offering from Love In Bloom Floral would be beautiful.

Cindy hung back behind the excited group of single girls, mostly teen and college age, and the other four Candy Canes, of course. But, they and she were more mature and didn't jiggle and giggle and act crazy. She raised her arms and waved her hands, more obligatory than really expecting to catch. She was watching Doreen. What a gift it would be for her to catch the flowers. Or, Natalie, who struggled financially with her small independent health club, or Candy, divorced and job seeking. She sought each one with her eyes, hoping for them. Not that catching the proverbial wedding bouquet really held the promise tradition claimed. But, it would be nice for any of them to have the special moment. Where she wondered was Connie?

The designer of Noelle's gorgeous wedding gown.

She heard cheers and screams and felt something in her hands. Two girls who she didn't know hugged her fiercely and jostled her. What! She hadn't even tried, but the bouquet of red striped Candy Cane roses was in her hands. She felt her face heat up. How did that happen? Noelle's back was to the group as she flung the bouquet over her head. But, Cindy knew even if she had been facing the group of women, she couldn't have planned it. She was a great swimmer, but a notoriously bad aim in softball and basketball. What did this mean that she had caught the bouquet and Rob the garter?

Congratulations! You have read Noelle's Christmas Wedding, the first in the Candy Cane Series. Did you get a kick finding out who Santa Claus was? It really wasn't too hard, was it? Hopefully it was fun and the Christmas party was, too.

The **Candy Cane** series will give you personal glimpses of Newport Beach, California from offbeat beaches to the village of Corona del Mar (where Cindy and Rob fall in love in a parking lot), and transport you back and forth to Scottsdale, Arizona.

**Cindy's story** is complicated with emotions and faith tugging at her heart. I hope you enjoy how she uses her faith and friendship with her **Promise Sisters** to deal with her love for Robinson and overcome her fears. They are a special couple who get married on a beach. Oops! Did I give too much away? Costa Rica is special to me because our son, Brian, and his adorable family lives right on the beach in Playa Hermosa where he surfs every day. We visited there several times when Brian pulled a coconut from a tree, poked a hole in it and let his sons Fletcher and Huxley drink from it. Moments like this are special in Costa Rica and **Cindy's story**.

Please keep reading to learn how **Candy** overcomes her fears and her life decisions. Will she take back her ex and go for her mother's advice?

To see all my other books please go to my website www.bonnieengstrom.com. All my books are different and fun, but romance grabs your heart in each. I appreciate reviews on Amazon and Goodreads – honest, short ones are great! Reviews encourage other readers and boost an author's standing.

You can also sign up for my quarterly newsletter on my website www.bonnieengstrom.com to learn about new releases and my latest writing endeavors.

Thank you.

Bonnie ~ who loves her readers.

PS ~ For my Newport Beach and Southern California readers … If there are any location inaccuracies, please remember this is a work of fiction, and I may have taken some allowances with venues and times.

    I can be reached at my email bengstrom@hotmail.com (be sure to put the word book in the subject line); via my website www.bonnieengstrom.com and my author page on Face Book. I love to hear from my readers, so please contact me.